The Cynthia Morgan Story

The Novel of Two Souls Predestined to be Together

Pat Gillespie

iUniverse, Inc.
New York   Bloomington

iUniverse books may be ordered through booksellers or by contacting:

iUniverse
1663 Liberty Drive
Bloomington, IN 47403
www.iuniverse.com
1-800-Authors (1-800-288-4677)

Because of the dynamic nature of the Internet, any Web addresses or
links contained in this book may have changed since publication and
may no longer be valid. The views expressed in this work are solely those
of the author and do not necessarily reflect the views of the publisher,
and the publisher hereby disclaims any responsibility for them.

ISBN: 978-1-4401-7055-3 (sc)
ISBN: 978-1-4401-7053-9 (hc)
ISBN: 978-1-4401-7054-6 (ebook)

Printed in the United States of America

iUniverse rev. date: 09/24/2009

Contents

Chapter One

"Good morning, all you sleepyheads, out there," the morning radio announcer called out at 6am, over Morgan's clock radio. "It is time for you who need to get up, to do so. And the best way I know how, is to put on some good ole' strong coffee, before grabbing that shower…"

"Mmmm… no…! Not yet!" the thirty-five year old, sandy blond haired, Gynecologist groaned, while running a hand over his tired face. "It seems like I just got to bed an hour ago."

"It was an hour ago," Catherine, his beautiful wife, in her last trimester of pregnancy moaned, while easing her way over into his arms, as he held them out to her.

"So much for getting my rest, before those two scheduled C-Sections today."

"Mmmm… I know. Last night's Emergency room must have really been packed. It was after four when you rolled into bed this morning."

"Yeah, it was. Did I wake you?" he asked, opening his hazel-green eyes to look down on her soft blonde hair, which smelled of sweet perfume.

"No, I wasn't able to sleep as usual. And as usual, our daughter is anxious to get out and join us," she smiled, while running her hand over her tummy.

"Well little one," he grinned, laying his hand over his wife's to talk to their unborn child,

"Doctor Burns says you are to behave yourself for another two and a half months. And the same goes for you, little one," he caringly reminded his thirty-three year old wife, with a smile, when they had been trying for several years to have a child. "I don't want to see either one of you get hurt. Much less, lose you."

"We'll be fine," she smiled warmly up at him.

"Catherine, I mean it," he groaned, looking into her glistening blue eyes.

"All right...! Now you had best be getting up," she softly laughed, while giving him a playful shove to get him out of bed. "It's getting late, and you still need to get yourself something to eat before you go."

"I can grab something on the way. Just let me get a shower first," he grinned, while carefully moving his arm from around her to get up.

"Good. Then that means I can stay in bed longer."

"Steve would prefer it."

"Yes, I know...!" she complained lightly.

Turning back to see the look on her sweet angelic face when she wrinkled up her nose at him, he smiled even more, and bent down to give her a kiss before doing the same to her well-rounded tummy. "Daddy loves you, baby girl."

"Yes, and so does mommy," Catherine cooed, while running hand over her husband's lean, muscular back, before he stood back up. "And so does mommy," she repeated with a heavy sigh.

Kissing her one more time, he hurried off to take his shower, so not to be too late for his two scheduled surgeries. "Hey!" he called out from their master bathroom. "What are you going to be doing today?"

"Resting for the most part. Though I would like to at least take a small shower to get freshened up," she returned, while attempting to sit up. Doing so, she suddenly became lightheaded, and reached out for the nightstand to study herself. "O...kay...!" she cried under her breath, so not to bring on any worry from her husband, when hearing the water being shut off. At which time, she made herself sit up more directly.

Coming out while toweling himself off, he detected something was wrong, when he saw the flushed look on her face just then. "Cat..." he called out, giving the towel a toss, while rushing over to check on her, "what is it?"

"Oh, it's nothing," she said, brushing his hand away. "I had probably just gotten up too fast, is all. Really."

"Are you sure that's all it is? Should I call Steve to have him come by and check on you? This could be leading up to something, you know."

"Yes. And if I have any more of these spells I'll call him," she assured him, when referring to one of their best friends, her doctor, and the one Morgan had taken over for the previous night, in the emergency room.

"All right, but just for the sake of argument, I'm going to call you every couple of hours to check on you myself," he announced, while getting to his feet to finish getting dressed.

Running her hand over her tummy, she wondered if indeed it was just that. *'Had I just gotten up to fast?'* Knowing her own mother, as well as all the other women down the line in her family, had died during childbirth, she sat, crying quietly, while he had his back to her. *'Is this my doom, as well?'* Looking over at his six-foot frame, with his beautifully trimmed hips and thighs, it nearly killed her to think she was going to meet with the same ending, having been the only child herself.

Unaware they were thinking the same thing, he stood poised, while looking back at her through the mirror on their dresser, he too cried, *'Please, Lord..., don't let this happen to her too. Not my Catherine and baby girl, please...!'*

Moments later, ready to head out, he walked back into the room. Seeing how she hadn't moved, he went back over to sit with her. "Are you sure you're all right?" he asked, placing an arm around her shoulder.

"Uh huh..." she cried, while laying her head against his chest.

"...All right," he conceded, taking in the scent of her long blonde hair, while holding her even closer, "if you are really sure, I won't press you then."

"Call me anyway!" she said, moving up to softly kiss his neck. Doing so, she knew how it would have an affect him.

"Mmmm..." he groaned deeply.

Pulling back, she caught the look of wanting in his eyes.

"Oh, girl, you are aching to keep me home, aren't you?" he grinned, looked over her heart shaped face, and then down to her small, but nicely shaped breasts.

"If only that were possible," she forced a smile up at him, just as one of her tears broke free to run down her cheek.

Catching it, he too wanted to cry, but knew it would only cause them both to worry needlessly, or so they had thought, as he went on to slowly kiss her. "I'll call you as soon as I can," he promised, as he went to get up. Stopping at the door, he turned back to smile one last time. "You know I really wish you would be careful today. Steve told me the other night that he real doesn't want you out of bed, if you don't have to be."

"I will. Now off with you," she continued to smile, while trying to keep a brave front on for him.

"Okay."

Turning, he was on his way out the door, and in his burgundy Chevy Tahoe in no time. Before starting it up, he stopped to look back at their red brick, ranch home, wondering if he should have called his friend anyway. "No, she would have told me if there was something wrong," he concluded, when starting up his vehicle to back out of their long driveway, of their tree-lined, street, in one of West Virginia, decent, hometown, neighborhoods.

After hearing him leave, she slowly got up, to go into the bathroom, to get a warm shower going. Getting there, she hadn't quite made it passed the sink, when feeling a sharp needle-like pain when her water broke.

Holding onto the sink, she looked back to see how far the phone was, when the real pain kicked in. "Oh, God, no_____!" she cried out, while waiting for it let up. When it had, she attempting to go back into their room to call her husband. However, doing so had only made it worse. "Ahhh_____! No! No! No!" she cried, through clinched teeth, while still having a hold of the sink. "Oh, God, why is this hap...pening to me_____? It hurts_____! It really..." she screamed, "hurts_____!"

As time painfully passed, things began to get quiet around her, as if sound itself had been taken away. Slowly then, she felt herself sliding down in front of the sink to the cold, ceramic, tiled floor below her.

Feeling her life, knowing it was about to slip away, she cried out again, only softly this time, "God_____ it...it's happening. It's really hap...pening, isn't it?" she sobbed, when feeling the tingling sensation around her mouth, as everything then started to fade. "No_____! Please_____ God, this c...can't be really hap...pening_____ to me_____!" she continued, while rocking her head back and forth to try to stay conscious. M...Morgan! Oh, Morgan, why did I have to go and tell you nothing was wrong? When..." she breathed in, and then slowly out, "something was wrong_____? Oh, God, M... Morgan_____!" her cries for him had only gotten quieter, as she began to fade in and out.

While still able to lean against the sink, visions started to flash before her, of the first day they had met in college. It was as if they were predestined for one another. On the other hand how, when time was working against her?

Praying hard he would sense she was in trouble, she continued weakly to cry out to him, though more subconsciously when she could.

Meanwhile, having arrived at the hospital, walking in, the first face Morgan saw was none other than Steve Burns himself.

"Hey, buddy!" the man in his mid-thirties called out, while standing at the nurses' station. "Why the long face?"

"Just tired," he replied, while going over to get out the two patients charts he would be working on that morning.

"Oh? And Cat, how is she?"

"She..." he started, when his thoughts went back to how she looked before leaving her.

"Morgan," his friend spoke up, as he went to place an arm around his shoulder, while holding a chart in the other hand, "I know you're worried about her, but I'm keeping a close eye on her. And knowing her history, well...!"

"Yeah, well that's what has me so worried. Steve," He pulled back in retaliation, "she looked as though she were about to pass out this morning."

"Oh? Did she say what might have caused it?"

"Something to do with getting up too soon. So she said."

"Well, then, stop worrying so." He patted him on the arm, and turned to get ready to go and see his first patient. "She'll call if she isn't feeling well!"

"Yeah, sure," he grumbled, as the two were about to go off in their own direction.

Then suddenly, feeling as if someone had called out to him, Morgan turned to see who it was. To his surprise, the area was cleared of all its workers. Not one nurse or doctor was anywhere to be seen. Not even Steve, who disappeared in one of the nearby rooms. "Great," he grumbled, as he was just about to turn and walk away, when it happened again.

"*Morgan...!*" the voice was that of his wife, reaching out to his conscious mind.

"Catherine...?"

"H...help me_____" she cried again.

"Cat_____?" he too cried, as a wave of panic hit him like a ton of bricks. "Dear, God! No_____!" he continued, while running back to grab the closest phone he could get his hands on, while tossing the charts onto the counter.

Having forgotten something, Steve came back and saw the look of horror on his friends' face. "Morgan, what is it?"

"Steve..." he cried, dialing his home, "something's wrong."

"How do you know?"

Not answering him, he waited, while tapping his hand on the counter, but there was no answer on the other end. "Damn...!" he growled.

"No answer?"

"No, and I've got this horrible feeling, she and the baby are in trouble."

"Then go to her. I'll get someone to cover for you, until you get back."

"Thanks," he called back over his shoulder, while running for the elevator. Just as the door was about to close, he stopped it. "Steve, I'll call you if she *is* in any trouble."

Waving his hand, Steve looked on worriedly, as the door to the elevator closed to one very traumatic-looking friend.

Moments later, after clearing the hospital parking garage, coming onto a busy intersection, he didn't want to wait on the light to turn green, when he ran it, while barely missing a car coming one way, and a utility van coming the other.

Seeing this, another one of his friends, Jason Gordon, being one of Cool Water's finest officers, spotted the Tahoe, boring down Main Street, at a rate of fifty miles an hour. Turning on his flashing lights, and siren, he immediately set off after him.

"Damn it, Jason," Morgan growled, as he looked back in his rearview mirror, when hearing the siren, "I can't stop now, Cat needs me." Just then, a thought came to him. In hopes his friend had his cell phone on him, Morgan reached for his own and quickly punched in his number.

The wait wasn't long, when Jason came over the other end. "Morgan, is that you?" he asked, seeing his name come over his phone.

"Yes, and damn it, Jason, Cat's in trouble. I have to get to her."

"In that case, let me by you. I can run on ahead and clear most of this traffic so you can get to her safely."

"Do it, buddy, but don't expect me to slow down. Nothing is going to keep me from getting to her. You copy that?"

"Yeah," he returned, hearing the pain in his voice to get to the woman he loves, "I copy that, buddy. Now I'm coming up on your left to go around you. So don't go and make any sudden lane changes." Doing so, he maneuvered the squad car around in no time, as the traffic up ahead moved over, seeing how something urgent was going on.

"Thanks, buddy," Morgan sighed heavily over his cell phone, before tossing it on the seat next to him.

"No problem, buddy," Jason had said more to himself, knowing the history of Catherine's family, too. "No problem."

Originating from New Orleans in the early part of the eighteen hundreds, her great-great-great-great grandmother Clarissa, started the line of fatal childbirths, as it kept on going through the line of Habersham women. While giving birth to a little girl, due to unanticipated complications, they would die, leaving their daughter to be raised by the father.

Meanwhile, reaching his home in less than the time normally taken, Morgan was out of his SUV, before his friend could reach his door handle.

Racing up to the front door, he didn't wait to unlock it, instead he threw his body into it, ripping the door halfway off its hinges.

"Cat_____!" he called out, running down the hall toward their room. "Cat_____!"

Reaching it, there was no sign of where he had last seen her.

"Cat_____!" he called out again, only quieter this time, as he rounded the corner of their master bath.

Stopping short of the doorway, he froze at what he saw lying limp on the floor in front of him. Then looking further, he saw a puddle of thick bodily fluids, traced with blood.

"Oh, God, no_____! Cat_____?" he cried, pushing himself away from the doorway to go to her.

Reaching her in one long stride, he knelt down, and quickly checked for her pulse, only to find it weak and barely readable.

"Cat_____?" he called out again, just as his friend rounded the doorway. "Jason..."

"Right here."

"Call for an ambulance. Now!"

"Done it, just after getting off the phone with you. I also took it upon myself to have them get a hold of Steve. He'll be on the ambulance, as well," he announced, seeing his friends' wife lying so still on the floor.

"And...?"

"They'll be here soon."

"Good. Until then, I have to do what I can."

"What have you been able to tell so far?"

"Without a doubt, her water sack has broken."

"That's not good, is it?"

"No," he stated, while reaching up for the towels from off the rack to elevate her head.

"What do you want me to do?"

"Get a blanket off the bed, and some more towels, while I check for signs of the baby."

"Got it," he returned, and rushed off to do just that.

In the meantime, rolling his wife carefully onto her back, he tearfully wiped her hair out of her face. "Cat... can you hear me...?" he called out, when hearing a faint moan come from her lips. "Cat...?"

"M...M...Morgan...!" she murmured weakly. "The ba...by...! She's c...coming...!"

"Now_____?" he asked, while going to look for himself.

"Ahhh_____" she cried, as he went to move her legs a part.

Seeing the crown of their daughter's head, he knew they were in trouble, when his wife began to slip in and out of consciousness.

"Cat_____! No_____!" he cried, looking up, when seeing her head drop off to one side. "Oh, Cat, no_____!" he continued, while reaching up to pull her back into his arms. Doing so, he felt what the cold bathroom floor was doing to her, and knew he had to get her out of there, and on to their bed.

"Jason, just toss those over to the side for now, we have to get her moved over to the bed. The cold floor is causing her to go into shock."

Losing his load, as Morgan carefully picked his wife up, Jason went over to quickly straighten up the bed, before Morgan got her there to lay her down as gently as he could.

Getting her covered, Morgan ordered Jason to go and see about the ambulance, while never once, taking his eyes off her. "Come on, Cat, beat this thing that has been going on in your family. Show them that you are not going to let it take you too. Come on_____ don't do this to me_____! Don't you dare do this to me. You hear me_____?" he sobbed, while dropping to his knees to cradle her in his arms. "Oh, God, please help us_____!"

Just as he continued to cradle her, the sound of an approaching ambulance pulled in out front.

Getting out first, Steve spotted the tall blond friend of theirs. "Jason, where are they?"

"Their bedroom," he announced, leading the way up to the front porch.

Seeing the mess Morgan had caused, when breaking down the front door, stopping to get around it, he asked, "Did Morgan do this?"

"Yes."

"Well this has to be gotten out of the way so we can get her out of here, and up to the hospital if we are to save her and the baby."

"I'll do that now. You know the way to their room, of course."

"Yeah. Guys..." Steve turned to the attendants, who were standing by with a gurney, "give him a hand, and then hurry on back to the last room on the right."

"Yes, Doctor Burns," they both returned, while hurrying to get the mess out of the way, as Steve went on back to Morgan's room.

Getting there, Morgan was just checking on the baby. "What do we have here?" Steve asked, coming around with his black bag in hand to see.

"I had just gotten her off the bathroom floor, and into bed, in hopes to warm her up so she wouldn't go into shock. Steve," he turned, looking all red-faced and crying, "the baby is coming. She's already crowning, and..."

"Morgan," He placed a hand on his friend's shoulder, "we'll do everything in our power to see this through. You and me, okay? For now, let's get your family out of here, and over to the hospital, where we have a team of the best waiting on us."

Seeing how they had no more time to waste, after checking her vitals, Steve took one last look at his friend.

Chapter Two

"I know, we have to hurry if we are to save them, but damn... where the hell is that gurney at?" he yelled, looking back at the door, once he got his composure back.

"Here, Doctor Fairbanks. We're here," one of the more stout male attendants announced, rushing in, while lugging all sorts of equipment on the gurney, as it rattled, and then struck the corner of the door frame, before making it through.

Once having done all they could for her there, placing her on the gurney, they quickly navigated it out through the tight-fitted doorway, before running down the hall, on out to the ambulance.

"Jason," Steve called out on their way to get her loaded up in the back of the ambulance, seeing how Morgan had enough on his mind, "secure the front door the best you can, will you?"

"Already on it," he returned from inside the house, where he put the door back into place, before sliding a heavy chair in front of it. Afterwhich, running out the back door, he locked it, and ran around front, in time to see them close the double doors to the ambulance, before racing off to the hospital.

Hurrying off to his squad car, Jason got in and soon took over the lead.

Meanwhile, inside the ambulance the two was doing everything they could to save her and the baby.

"Damn, this isn't good," Steve groaned frantically, when only able to get a faint reading of her heartbeat. "Her heart rate is nearing the danger point as I speak."

Reaching up to place two hands on either sides of her face, Morgan called out to her, "Damn it, Cat, you can't do this to me, I need you!" he cried once again through tear-dampened eyes, "You hear me? Don't you go and die on me! Don't you dare go and..."

"M...Morgan...?" she whispered faintly, cutting him off, "I...I... l...love you_____!"

"M...Muffet..." he cried, not knowing where that came from, "I...I l...love you too!"

"Catherine," Steve interrupted, "It's me, Steve. Try to hang in there, girl. We're almost there," he called out, seeing how she was about to pass out again. "Come on, girl..., you got to hang in there."

"Steve_____!" Morgan cried out, not able to find her pulse.

Lifting one of her eyelids, they had their answer.

"Damn it... no_____!" Morgan shouted, when the two began CPR, just as her heart had given out completely.

"One and two and three and four," Steve counted out the compressions, while Morgan handled the breaths.

After going at it for a brief time, Morgan checked for a pulse at the side of her neck.

"Anything?" Steve asked.

"No, not yet," he answered mournfully.

"Damn it, Morgan, I would suggest using the defibrillator, but I'm afraid what that might do to the baby."

"Then let's try the CPR again."

Doing so, within the second breath, Morgan felt a faint response coming from her, as the ambulance reached the hospital.

Pulling up, they didn't take any unnecessary time to get the doors open, when rushing Catherine inside to be prepped and ready for what was sure to be a life-threatening crisis.

"Steve?" Morgan cried, looking to his friend.

"Come with me," he ordered, taking his arm. "You know though, this is going against all hospital regulations. However, under the circumstances, I'm going to need your help. But only if you can keep your head."

"Just tell me what you want me to do."

"Get suited up, and let's try and save your wife and baby."

Try they did. After hours of one scare after another, the baby was delivered, but only to survive for a brief hour, before her monitor went into a flat line.

As for Catherine, she had only come to for a brief, but tear jerking moment, as she looked to her husband, and cried, "Morgan_____ remember_____"

"Cat, no_____! Please_____ no_____!" he cried, painfully, knowing now that he was going to lose her. "Please_____ don't go_____!"

"Oh, but I'm not ever going to leave you...! It's fate...! Somewhere, when you least expect it... we will meet again. And M...Morgan..." she held out long enough to get the last of her farewells out, "I will... a...always... I...love... you_____"

"Cat_____" he cried out, just as her monitor went off, "Ca_____therine_____!

No_____!" he carried on painfully. "Oh, God, No_____!"

"Get the paddles in here!" Steve called out, pulling his friend away.

Trying everything they could to bring her back, it was useless.

Stepping forward, as everyone there moved aside, Morgan brought her up into his arms, and held her close. "Oh,

Cat_____" he sobbed, burying his face into her hair, "why_____?"

Giving him that moment, Steve turned to the others and signaled them to leave the two alone, while one of the nurses tended to the deceased infant.

Shortly thereafter, Steve returned to take his friend out of there so they could take care of her remains. "Morgan, it's time now, buddy. She's gone to be with your little girl."

"But why, Steve? Why her? And why the baby? That's not how it had happened in the past!"

"I wish I could answer that, but I don't know. Perhaps the answer lies somewhere in her past. Have you really checked into it?"

"No. We were just hoping it was some kind of a fluke. Maybe in the gene pool, and had hoped this time she would have been spared."

"Well, knowing she was the last of her family, there will be no more like this happening."

"You're right," he was saying, when turning to see a nurse and two orderlies about to cart his wife and infant away. "Wait," he called out, stopping them.

"Doctor Fairbanks," the nurse nodded respectfully. "Guys," she turned to the two and instructed them to pull back and let Morgan in to say his goodbyes.

Just as he was about to, Steve's wife, Christy, an average brunette, in her mid-thirties, showed up, after getting a call from her husband. "Steve...!" she called out walking up.

Holding up a hand, she waited, while Morgan went up to uncover his daughter.

Looking down on his little girl, he tearfully kissed her tiny little hand. "I love you, my little Christina," he cried sadly. "I...l...love you...!"

Giving him an added second or two, Steve then motioned the nurse to go on with them, before he and his wife took Morgan home to mourn his loss privately.

"Morgan," Christy then came around to offer him a regretful hug, "I am so sorry about Cat and the baby," she said, pulling back to look up into his tear-dampened face, "And Lacy will be really heartbroken too, when she finds out about her Aunt Cat and baby Christina."

"Named after you," he returned, with a forced smile, while seeing the last of his family go, when the elevator doors closed.

"Hey," Steve spoke up, "I had already cleared away the rest of the day. How about we get you out of here, and home, where you can have some time to yourself."

"Yes, and I can see to Cat and Christie's things for the funeral this evening, if you want," Christy offered reverently.

"Thanks. She said you would know what she would have liked if something like this were to have happened."

"And the funeral," Steve mention hesitantly, "You don't have to worry about all that right now. We can help in any way you wish when the time comes."

"Thanks. There is so much to do, and so many to call. Right now I would like to take you on your offer and get out of here."

"Let's go then," Steve offered, leading the way.

On their way out, they passed by a lot of the staff members who heard about the tragedy, and wanted to offer their sympathy.

Getting down to the main lobby, they ran into the hospital Administrator, who came to offer his condolences.

"Morgan," the short, balding man in his mid-forties spoke up, "I just heard the news. Anything I can do to make this time go smoothly, just say the word."

"Thanks, Gerald, I wish I could say there is, but..." He broke off, walking away.

"Steve, Christy, let me know, won't you? You two are the closest he has as family, since his folks have passed a short while back."

"We'll be certain of it," Steve returned, shaking the man's hand before leaving.

Finding their friend outside, standing at the far end of the hospitals' courtyard, surrounded by dogwood trees and picnic tables, they walked up just as a few nurses walked away.

"I can't do this anymore," he said, staring out over the well-landscaped pavilion.

"Do what?" Steve asked, coming up to stand in behind him.

"Operating rooms. I can't go back in there without thinking about what had just happened. I...it'll never be the same e...ever again."

"Morgan...!" Christy came up to stand by his side. "Honey, what you just gone through, no one would expect you to just go right back in there, as if nothing had happened."

"Give it time, buddy," Steve offered delicately, while resting a hand on his shoulder. "For now, let's get out of here."

Turning, Morgan looked back on the hospital one last time, when having made up his mind never to step foot in it again.

That night, staying at Steve and Christy's stone and sided bi-level house, Lacy, their twelve-year old was told of Cat's passing.

"And the baby too...?" she cried.

"Yes, sweetie, the baby too," her mother replied, while having to fight from losing her tears once again, after getting back from Morgan's place with the things for the funeral. One being the soft blue, silky-like dress Cat had talked about. And the other, a pretty pink, yellow, and white taffeta, Morgan's mother made for the baby, before she passed away, after learning they were going to be having a girl.

Not wanting to bother her uncle, Lacy went to her room to cry it out.

As for Morgan, getting settled into the guest room, sleep wasn't going to be that easy, when dreams of his beloved came back to haunt him. Dreams that also stemmed around her last statement she made to him about always being with him. *"Oh, but I'm not ever going to leave you...! It's fate...! Somewhere, when you least expect it... we will meet again. And M...Morgan... I will... a... always... l...love... you_____!"* Love you... love you... love you... love you... The thought echoed in his head, until he had to get up to get some fresh air.

Doing so, he dressed in a pair of sweats Christy packed for him, along with other things he would need from his house, and then pulled on a pair of running shoes. When he was done, he headed out for a long brisk run to clear his head.

Not knowing where he was going to run, he found himself standing in his own front yard, two miles away from his friends' house, in the early morning dew.

"Great. Just where I didn't want to end up," he grumbled painfully, dropping to his knees. Balling up fists, he tried not to cry, but before it was over, he had pulled up hand full of grass, aching to have the whole day to do over again. Only this time, he would not have gone in, but called his friend instead, or took his wife in to have her checked out.

"Why couldn't I have done that_____?" he cried, not realizing he wasn't alone.

"Would it have made any difference?" came a voice from behind, while getting off the phone with their friend.

"What?" Morgan turned to see Jason pocket his cell phone, while crossing the street from where he had his black Chevy pickup parked to watch the house.

"Would it have made any difference? Aside from having that extra bit of time with her, would it have made any difference?" he repeated.

Coming to a stop in front of him, Morgan saw his own tears. When having been friends, since grade school, and then college, Cat had become like a sister to him as well. "I'm sorry, I didn't know you were there. I guess her passing would have hit you pretty hard too, huh?"

"Yeah, it did. And so you know, I just called Steve to let him know you were here, and that I'll be bringing you back. When you are ready to go, that is."

"Thanks. And yes, to have what bit of time I could have with her, I would gladly take it."

Turning back, they looked at the house when then a patrol car went slowly by.

"Is everything all right?" the middle-aged officer asked, not realizing who it was standing there in the dark. "Jason... is that you?"

"Yes, Jim, and Morgan too."

"Doctor Fairbanks, sorry I didn't realize it was you, Sir. Sorry about your loss. A lot of us are down at the station."

"Thanks."

"Well, I'll be going. Take care," he waved, and pulled away.

"I'm glad to have people like that watching my place," he laughed, knowing from the looks of it, Jason had been parked across the road for some time, before he showed up.

"You know, don't you?" Jason asked, running a hand over his hair.

"You? Sitting over there? Watching my place? Not at first! But then, I don't recall hearing you pull up either."

"Yeah, well it's getting late, and you have a lot to do these next few days. So how about I give you that ride back to Steve's if you're ready?"

Taking one last look, back at the house, with all the trees scattered about the front and side lawn, he agreed. "Let's go."

Heading across the road to get into the passenger side of his friends' truck, before he could, he had to move all the fast food wrappers that were in his way.

"Gees, Jason, is all this just from tonight?"

"Yeah, well..."

They laughed, and headed out.

Chapter Three

The next few days, family and friends got together to say their tear-filled goodbyes.

Not seeing the tall, reddish-blond haired man in his thirties, come strolling up behind him, Morgan felt the warmth of yet another friends' hand lay lightly on his shoulder.

"Hey there. You have time for a long lost friend, about now?" he asked, grinning, when Morgan turned to see another college roommate, grinning at him.

"Nate... Winslow...?" he cried out in surprise. "When did you get here?"

"When Steve called right after she and the baby died. Man, Morgan, I'm so sorry to hear about her and the baby," he offered, as tears welled up in his eyes.

"Yeah, well..." he groaned, while turning to look sadly at what was to have been his family, "what am I to do now? She's all I ever wanted."

"You still have no idea what caused it to begin with, do you?" he asked, looking on at the two peaceful people in their beautiful caskets. Catherine in a satiny snow-white number, wearing a soft blue, cottony, dress, while holding a beautiful handmade flower arrangement Lacy had made for her. Then little Christina, sweet, and angelic, just like her mother. Though, even as tiny as she was lying there in her little infant casket, he was surprised to see the soft ringlets of blonde hair on her sweet little head. "Morgan," Nate didn't wait for his answer, when admiring the tiny infant casket, "who did all this?"

"Steve, Christy, and Lacy. I picked out the caskets," he smiled tearfully at how his little girl's was done up in heavenly pink satin, with clouds of angels hovering overhead, while hand-painted puppies and kittens romped around each one.

"And the dresses?" He couldn't help but admire even more, particular that of the baby's.

"Cat had it all picked out when we were talking about how her mother and her mother's mother passed before her. That, and mom made Christina's for her, just before she passed away a few months ago. Funny thing, she had hoped to have been here when she heard we were going to have a girl."

"And your dad, having died of cancer, before that."

"Yeah. Anyway, what were you asking me before this?"

"How she had died."

"No, I don't know. But I'll be damned if I don't find out."

"Hey, that reminds me."

"What?" Morgan turned to see the look on his friends' face.

"Well, if you're wanting to get down to the bottom of this. That would mean one thing!"

"Go to New Orleans?"

"Yes!"

"And since your practice is there? No. I'm sorry," he shook his head, "but after losing Cat, I am thinking about leaving my practice. Like I had told Steve the other day, I can't go back into another operating room after seeing her die right there in my arms. Sorry, pal, I can't do that.

Not anymore."

"Oh, but I'm not one of you," he laughed.

"What…?"

"No! After we went our separate ways, I went back and finished off a whole other course, and joined the ranks of the big V," he grinned broadly.

"You what...?" Morgan asked, gleaming into his friends' shinning blue eyes. "You're a...a..."

"Veterinarian?" he smiled. "Yep! And loving it, too. Heck, think about it, horses are greatly raised down there, not just in Kentucky."

"Yes, but I thought being a doctor was what you wanted."

"Yes, well that was then."

"What changed your mind?"

"After getting set up with my general practice, I came across this old veterinarian that was about to retire. Man, he had this huge practice and didn't want to see it go to waste. So he offered it to me if I would simply finish off a few extra courses and agree to take it over."

"So you did?"

"Yep! And boy, I could really use you down there. In fact, remember that old plantation we almost saw, while the two of you were down last?"

"I recall something about it. But to tell you the truth, I haven't given it much thought lately."

"Well it may be coming available. Not to mention, it's in real need of some fixing up. Oh, and of course, that's if you don't mind a few ghosts living with you."

"Ghost...? Yeah, right, you're out of your mind. You know I don't believe in that sort of stuff."

"Yeah, well wait until I remind you what the name of the place is."

Before he could tell him, a few of the guests walked up to offer their condolences, before walking away crying.

"Listen," Morgan leaned over quietly, while seeing his other friends carry on with a few other town's people, "how about we get out of here? I need some air, and to get away from all this sad music they're playing."

"Sure! What did you have in mind?" he asked, before Morgan went up to say goodbye to his loved ones, before heading out.

"Anywhere, but here," Morgan groaned.

"Okay," he agreed, hanging back to give his friend time to place a kiss on his fingertips, before lightly touching them to his wife's lips, and then to his daughter's cheek.

"I'll be back before…" he broke off tearfully at the thought of having to say his final goodbyes.

Seeing this, Nate went up to take his arm, knowing how much he needed a friend. "Hey, come on, let's go and get that fresh air. What do you say, huh?"

Doing so, Nate led the way toward the door of the luxurious funeral home, when Steve and Jason walked up.

"Where you two off to?" Steve asked, quietly.

"Just out to get some fresh air," Morgan replied through tear-dampened eyes. "Would you mind sticking around to see to the others?"

"Yes, sure," he said, turning to grin at Nate. "Take care of him."

"Oh, yeah, sure I will."

Heading on out, the two went to their own vehicles, before deciding where they wanted to go.

"Hey, what do you say about the Roy's Diner?" Nate called out.

"You remember that old place?"

"Of course!" he called back, laughing about their old hang out that once had a juke box in it, playing records for a quarter. But that was more their parents time, until someone brought them back for a while to see if it would work out.

Remembering all the fun they had, when the place used to have curb service, he was all for it, knowing it had been a thing of the past for quite awhile. "Yeah, sounds good."

Getting into his Tahoe, he went to start it up, but then stopped, when he saw the first signs of April rain hitting his windshield. *Oh, Cat…* he cried, laying his head on the steering wheel for a brief moment, before starting it up, and pulling out.

Once they had arrived at the old log cabin-looking diner, the two went in, where once again Morgan was greeted by other mourners. Keeping it brief, they went to get seated at a corner table, where they could talk more privately.

"And now, what were you saying about the name of this place?" Morgan asked, after giving an older waitress their order.

"Are you ready for this?" his friend asked with a mischievous smile.

"Nate, out with it."

"Well, first let me just tell you a little bit about the place. It had belonged to an old sea

Captain, named Thaddeus Morgan. Does any of that ring a bell?" Not giving Morgan time to reply Nate went on, "Well anyway, his wife had died giving birth to a little girl, named Cynthia, back in the late eighteen hundreds. Now, from what I'm told, he was a real tyrant after that, and would never allow his daughter to lift a finger to do anything. Oh, but don't get me wrong, he loved her all right. But then, when it came time to allow in any kind of suitors, he wouldn't hear of it, and would always chase them off, or had his hired hands to do it for him. Then one day, with all that was going on with the thoroughbreds being raised around there, not to mention, his own breed of Morgans, of all kinds to be raising..."

"Maybe it was a joke," Morgan teased, while listening on.

"Yeah, well, at the time people were paying big bucks to use them as work horses, along with the usual stock they used. And because of it, he had to go and hire himself a veterinarian to tend to them."

"Is that what he did in the way of making a living?"

"Oh, no, not him. After taking an early retirement from the sea, he went on to banking, and made it big doing so. But then, it ran on his side on the family."

"So money had always been there for him. And his wife, what of her side of the family?"

"Oh, yeah, and hers as well! As of right now, the attorneys are looking for any remaining family to pass the estate over to. However, if no one can be found, they will have no choice but sell it."

"Who's been taking care of it all this time?"

"All I know is Doc. Ramsey, after his father had died years ago."

"And now, the name?"

"What else?" he laughed. "The Morgan Plantation, after Captain Morgan, himself!"

"And that's why you thought of me?"

"Sure! Heck, don't you remember how Cat and I use to razz you about the place? Saying how it had been named after you."

Shaking his head, he mused over the story, while taking a drink of his coffee.

"Oh, and there's more."

"What?" he asked, when his friend turned to look off at all the people that were enjoying the old hometown feel of their surroundings. "Nate," Morgan barked to get him to snap out of it, and go on with the story, "I'm waiting. What else is there?"

"Oh, yeah, well it was said that young Cynthia had fallen in love with the veterinarian, who had also been a sea Captain, like dear ole' dad. How could she have gone wrong, you might ask. Well, daddy didn't approve. And worse yet, she had become..."

"Pregnant?"

"Oh, yeah."

"Damn..."

"Yes, well they wanted to marry, but daddy had him killed, when he discovered it."

"And the baby?"

Nate didn't know how to tell him.

"Well...?"

"Morgan..."

"Spit it out. What was it?" he growled.

"...A girl."

He glared at him at first, and then shook his head. "Oh, Christ, you're not going to tell me that she too..."

"Died, while giving birth. Like her mother, and her mother's mother before her?"

"What? Just like Cat's family?"

"Yeah, what a coincidence, huh?" He cringed, when looking down at his cup, waiting to see what Morgan was going to say next.

"I just wonder..." he stopped to think.

Looking back up, he was surprised. However, knowing more about her past from this Doctor Ramsey, friend, he asked anyway if he thought there could be a connection.

"Exactly. Listen, it's getting late and I need to be getting back and seeing to the others. Where are you staying?"

"The Hilton."

"Why so far away?"

"It's the best I could do in such short notice."

"Fine. Call me in the morning. I will know more then on what I am going to do. As for your offer, it sounds tempting. Just let me talk it over with the others, and I will let you know what I have decided. Besides, I have a meeting with the lawyer to go over some paperwork. It seems that he has received some sort of a letter from a law firm down your way, and wishes to discuss it with me."

"Oh, yeah?"

The look on his friend's face said it all about the old plantation, when he broke out laughing. "No way. That would have to be one very long shot. And in the dark even yet!"

"Oh, well, you can't blame me for hopin'! Think about it though, you, owning such a magnificent estate, once it gets fixed up to its original beauty," he teased, knowing about the other law firm. "Oh, and by the way, they never found her lover's body, either."

"Great. So what you're saying is that he's probably the one haunting the place."

"No. That would be her father."

"And the other?"

"Oh, well, who knows," he laughed.

Though he did know, as he had been told, not only by Ramsey, but by an old local psychic, who had been waiting for something to happen, connected to the plantation. What she told him was the spirit of the young woman had been haunting the place. However, while waiting for her lost love to return, she didn't know her father had him killed. Then some time ago, it was said that she had stopped her hauntings unexpectedly. Although, while she *was* there, her father's spirit always tried to keep a tight grip on her.

'Perhaps that's the reason for her silence in such a long time.' Nate thought when the two were finishing up.

"Hey, why so quiet?" Morgan asked, while the two went to pay the bill.

"Just thinking, is all."

Walking out of the diner, the two said their goodnights and parted company, while Morgan headed back to the funeral home, where he saw the others off.

Going back to his place, when having decided to sleep on the couch, Morgan made a few phone calls, before turning in. When he did fall off to sleep, more dreams haunt him. Dreams he could not quite understand. Like why he called his wife, Muffet. And horses running in fields as far as the eye could see.

Chapter Four

By morning, getting up to use the main bathroom, Morgan got
himself ready for his meeting with their lawyer, which was to
take place at the same diner he and Nate were at the previous
day.

Getting through with his shower, he went back into the
bedroom to change, but stopped to look at the closed bathroom
door. Recalling the horrible incident that took place there, he
felt his knees about to give out, when he sat down heavily on
their bed. "Oh, Cat_____" he cried again, this time, into
doubled up fists, "why you_____? Why_____?" he growled
heatedly, before throwing on his jeans and pullover sweater.

Grabbing his tennis shoes, he went out to the living room
to put them on, before going out the door to head over to the
diner. Stopping though, something didn't seem right, when
turning to look back at the room. Then it dawned on him; one
of his friends must have fixed the front door. He laughed then,
and headed on out.

Reaching the diner, he spotted their lawyer, a distinguished-
looking, middle-aged man with thinning brown hair, sipping
coffee, while looking over some briefs. "Ted...!" Morgan called.

"Morgan," the man looked up warmly. "How are you doing?"
he asked, getting up to offer him a seat across from him.

Standing just about the same height, the two shook hands, before going on to take their seats and order their breakfast.

"Ask me in about a year or two," he groaned, while accepting a cup of coffee from the usual red headed waitress that had always waited on him in the past. "Thanks, Tracy."

"Your welcome, Doc.," the twenty-two year old smiled thoughtfully. "Are you wanting the usual today?"

"Yes, and whatever he's wanting, just put it on one bill."

"Sure thing."

After Ted placed his order, he went about getting out the papers needed for their meeting. "Now, here is what I have for you. It isn't much since everything reverts over to you anyway. And am I correct to assume that the burial is today, too?"

"Well, possibly. However, there has been a slight change as to where."

"What? What sort of change?"

"I'm taking her down to New Orleans, where she would have wanted to go if we would have moved down there awhile back. And since her family had originated from there, it's only fitting that she'd be there with them."

"But what about you? This is your home!"

"Not after this passed week," he explained with difficulty.

"What...?"

"No. I'll be leaving my practice, and taking Nathaniel Winslow up on his offer."

"Nathaniel? Why isn't that one of your old college friends, along with Steve Burns?"

"Yes, and there's more."

"Oh?"

Laughing, he explained the change in his friends' career, from general practice to taking over a well-established veterinary clinic for a retired doctor.

"Well, I'll be. What a change that must have been. Why, you three had it all worked out, in how you were all going to open an office down there. But then you and Steve got an offer up here instead, leaving your friend to his own practice there."

"Yes, and I felt bad doing that. But then…"

"You met your wife at college, and you two fell madly in love?"

"Madly is right. The first time I saw those eyes of hers, it was as if we had known each other a long time ago."

"In another life?" he asked, raising an eyebrow.

"What, reincarnation?" he smirked.

"Well…?"

"First, Nate springs something on me about ghosts in an old plantation house, and now you? What next?" he choked, sipping on his coffee.

"What about an old plantation house?" Ted asked, immediately picking up on the subject.

"Oh, some estate down in New Orleans," he said with a flip of his hand, while looking into his cup. "In fact it was named…"

"The Morgan Plantation?" he asked, cutting him off.

"Yes, why?"

Pulling out a letter he had gotten, he felt apprehensive at first about giving it to him, having read it himself. "I don't quite know how to tell you this, so I'll just give this to you and have you read it yourself."

"What is it?"

"Something that came in the mail the other day. After going over it, I thought it had to be some sort of fluke. Then taking in the facts of your late wife's history, it started to make sense."

Taking it, he looked to the man across from him. "What is this about?"

"Your wife's past."

Seeing the postmark from New Orleans, he knew his search for her past was now in his hands. Upon opening it, his hands began to shake, as he read the first few lines. "This can't be true," he claimed, gesturing a hand at the page.

"I'm afraid it is. I called them myself to confirm their findings. And..."

"They're crazy. The Morgan Plantation?"

"Yes. It seems that recently, they received a call from some unknown source after they put out several notices in all the major papers across the country. After hearing about your wife's passing, and about her history, they began an extensive background check on her, and, well...!"

"An extensive background check, and they came up with this? Some check! She hadn't been gone all that long. How could they have done such a thorough check, being that it has only been a few days? And just who is this caller? Some nut ball wanting to get his name in all the papers?"

Before he could answer, Morgan's friend walked up, hearing the last part of their conversation. "No," he put in solemnly.

"What?" Morgan turned to see the look on his friends' face, when walking up. "And just how did you know to find me here?"

"Steve. He called to talk the other night, when I got back to my room. As for this, I..." he began, when the waitress came back with their order.

"Will you be joining them?" she asked.

"Morgan?" Nate turned sadly to look to his friend.

"Yes."

"Put it on your bill, as well?" she asked.

"No..." Nate started up, but only to be cut off.

"Put it all on my bill!" the lawyer exclaimed.

"Ted, that isn't necessary," Morgan protested. "I can cover it."

"No. It's done. Now let's all take our seat and see what your friend, here, has to say on the matter."

Doing so, Nate sat down next to his friend, but did not offer an explanation right away, until after the waitress had brought him some coffee.

Not able to wait much longer, Morgan pushed forward, "Nate, what did you mean by that comment just then?"

"Only that it was me who made the call to the law firm."

"What?" he asked.

"Yes, right after reading about the plantation in the papers, and then getting the call from Steve. Heck it all began to make sense."

"So," the lawyer spoke up, "you're the informant?"

"Yes."

"And what all we talked about yesterday, you knew all along?" Morgan asked, feeling betrayed.

"Well, not everything."

"Meaning?" he growled.

"They never called me back to tell me that she was the missing link. I was just, well... teasing."

"Teasing...?" Morgan half laughed. "Of all times you decide to joke around, you picked one hell of a time to do it now!" he shook his head.

"Morgan, I'm sorry! Please! I know how much she meant to you. And well, after Steve called and told me how she had died..."

"You had to call them and see, didn't you?"

"Well, Steve said you needed answers, and after our talk the other day, I was right to do so. Oh, sure I should have talked it over with you first, but time was of the essence."

"Essence, huh? More paranormal talk, Nate?"

"Well...!"

"Nate...!" he growled.

"Yes, well, there is this old woman, a psychic, who has been keeping tabs on the place ever since there had been talk about hearing some ghosts wondering about it."

"Nate, no more about these ghosts! I don't believe in them."

"All right! But have you considered my offer? Will you come down and give me a hand? You and Steve both, that is?"

"You've asked Steve, too?"

"Yes. Well, no. Not actually."

"Which is it? Yes or no?"

"No. I wanted to see what you would say, before going to him about it."

Still shaking his head, he looked down into his half filled cup, before looking over at his lawyer, who already knew of his decision.

"Morgan, please... say you will come. Besides, it will be great having the three of us, and yes, even Christy, and Lacy there."

"Nate..."

"No, Morgan, please...!" his friend interrupted, while continuing to beg. After years of separation, he had come to missing his old friends.

Pulling out his cell phone, Morgan looked once more at his lawyer, and just grinned, as he punched in Steve's number. Afterward, he handed the phone over to his friend.

"What?" Nate asked, baffledly.

"If you're going to ask him, you had best be doing it now, don't you think?" he smiled.

Hearing Steve's voice over the other end, Nate went on about their plans. Though, not long after, he turned back to the others and asked, "Would it be all right if they were to join us for coffee?"

"Sure," Morgan replied, looking to Ted.

"That's fine by me. Besides, I shouldn't be too much longer here. I have to get back to the office before the funeral."

"Great," Morgan returned.

Getting through with the call, Nate handed the phone back, while the lawyer was having Morgan sign a few papers, one of which was the document from the other law firm.

"And now that that's taken care of, I'll see you two later," he announced, while slipping the papers back into his briefcase.

"All right," Morgan stood and shook his hand.

After his departure, the two sat quietly for a few minutes, before uttering a word. Then finally, Nate spoke up first, "Steve laughed at first about the idea."

"Oh?"

"Yeah, but then I reminded him about our first conversation back in college."

"And?"

"Well, he's interested. He said things wouldn't be the same without you here."

"Yeah, well, it would be hard to say goodbye."

'*No, doubt,*' Nate thought more to himself, while enjoying the rest of his meal.

A short time passed, when the two looked up to see Steve and his wife walking in, all smiley faced.

"Well, does this mean what I think?" Morgan grinned.

"Well, we have certainly talked it over," Steve grinned.

"And Lacy, how did she take it?" he asked.

"Our girl?" Christy smiled. "She's over bragging to her two best friends about it now!"

"All right!" Nate cried, happily. "Now as to where you will be staying."

"Nate...!" Morgan shot him a warning look.

"But it would be perfect."

"No. At least not until I have a chance to check it out. And then, I'm only saying, if there is any truth to what you had said about the place, I'm not all that sure it would be suitable for the rest of them."

"What place is that?" Steve asked, while taking off his jacket, before helping his wife off with hers.

"The old Morgan Estate," he explained.

"You mean, Plantation," Nate corrected, teasingly.

"Nate...!" he warned again.

"All right...! Man, you still have to be the tough one out of the three of us, don't you?"

"With reason, my friend. With reason."

Getting their coffee and tea ordered, the four went on talking about the upcoming move.

"I can have Ted take care of my place, and yours, as well, if you two would like," Morgan offered Steve and Christy quietly.

"And Cat? What about her and your little girl?" Christy asked.

"They're going, too. It has all been arranged already."

"Since when?" Steve sounded surprised.

"Since last night, after leaving you two."

"Oh...?" his friend was still sounding puzzled.

Seeing this, he went on, "Yeah, just after the final showing, I'm having them flown down to be buried at the Memorial Park Cemetery, where I was assured there were other Habersham women buried there, and I might add, in a pretty big family plot."

"And you are sure they are the same family?" Christy asked, sounding uneasy.

"Yes. The park manager knows the story quite well from what he has told me. And now, to learn that the old Morgan Plantation was a part of her heritage, as well?" he questioned.

"What a jolt!" Steve offered his friend, sadly, while looking down at his watch. "Hey, hate to end such a warm fuzzy moment, but don't we have to be at the funeral home soon?"

"Yeah, you are right!" Morgan agreed, checking his watch. "I have just enough time to get changed and head on over."

With the bill having been taken care of, the four filed out of the diner one by one.

"Listen, since I have to get changed first, how about I just meet you all over there?"

"Sure!" they agreed, looking to one another.

After Morgan walked out, the others wondered if he shouldn't be left alone at a time like this.

"No, he shouldn't be alone right now," Nate agreed, while looking out at his friend, standing by this SUV.

"No, one of us should tag along, in case he needs us," Steve agreed.

"I'll go," Nate suggested. "The two of you still have to go and get Lacy yet."

"You're right. So we'll see you two there," the two agreed, while heading out into the bright sunlit day to go and get what they had to, before going to the final showing.

Chapter Five

After the showing ended, everyone left, but Morgan, who stayed behind to linger over what all he was going to be missing.

"Morgan?" Christy spoke up softly from the doorway.

Not answering, he turned his head back slightly to acknowledge his silent reply.

"Would you like for us to take care of her things for you, while you fly down ahead of us? We will see to it too that the Tahoe gets there, as well!"

"Yes, that's fine. Just pack it all and bring it with you. I will take it from there, if that's all right with the two of you?"

"Sure!" Steve added, just as he went up to place an arm around his friends' shoulder. "We'll be there for you, buddy. Remember that."

"Yeah. What do you think it will take? A week? Maybe two?"

"We are probably looking at, at least two," he agreed.

With a nod of his head, they were gone, leaving Morgan to mourn alone. "Well, Cat..." He stood to walk over to her casket first, "it's how you would have wanted it! We are going to New Orleans, you and I, and our..." he stopped to look over at their little one, and with tears welling up in his eyes, he cried, "Lord... this wasn't how it was supposed to go...! We were supposed to be a family, the three of us! And now..." he went on, while looking back down upon his wife, "she at least gets to be with her other family! As for this plantation house, I don't know about that. It was hers to have, not mine...!" he sobbed in silence, until he felt the presence of the clergy standing at the door.

"Mr. Fairbanks, anytime you are ready, Sir! We had just gotten a call from the airport, telling us that they would like to have the two loaded and ready, just as soon as you are."

"Of course," he sniffled quietly, before saying yet another goodbye, as he went to place a warm kiss to his finger tips again, as he had done the night before to her lips, and the same to his little girl's cheek, yet when he choked back another sob, while saying goodbye. "Oh, Lord, how I loved you both..." he cried mournfully, before having to force himself away so that they could be taken to the airport.

Meanwhile, time had gone by slowly, with Morgan home packing for his trip, Steve and his family stopped by, along with Jason, who was thrown by the news of his leaving so abruptly.

"I can't believe it, will I ever see you again?" he asked, sadly.

"Sure you will. And don't be alarmed if I call you from time to time."

"Well, I sure hope so! And listen, a bit of warning that I happened to have heard over the wire."

"Oh? You sound worried. What's up?"

"It is about those thoroughbreds. You want to watch out for a man name Copeland. He's bad news around there."

"Oh, what are we talking?" Steve asked.

"He hates to lose races. Meaning, he will do anything to make certain he never does."

"Anything?" Morgan asked.

"Anything. Moreover, his father wasn't any different. He was just as power hungry, and to prove it, they found some unlucky stiff's skeleton with Vincent Copeland's name on it. Jewish too, they said."

"How would they know that, if he was a skeleton?" Morgan asked sarcastically. "Did they have some kind of test to show he had been circumcised?"

They all laughed.

"No. He was found with a crucifix around his neck."

"Great, I will pass that on to Nate, when I see him at the airport later. Meanwhile, I had better be getting my stuff put together if I am to catch that flight on time."

"Sure. I'll be waiting to hear from you," Jason said, saying his goodbyes.

After seeing him off, with the help of the others, Morgan had an old navy trunk loaded with mostly his things, and a few of hers to remember her by.

"Uncle Morgan," Lacy called out from the doorway, when he and her father went to carry the big, black, trunk out, "wouldn't you like to take this with you?" she asked, tearfully, while holding up a special teddy bear, which she had made for the baby.

Seeing the multi-colored bear in her hand, followed by tears rolling down her cheek, he looked to Steve, before setting the trunk down to walk up to her. "Sure I would," he smiled, while giving her a hug. "It would mean a lot to me to have this with me."

"You mean it? You're not just saying that, are you?"

"No!" He pulled back to look down into her twelve year old face. "It's just hard for me to go into her room, knowing that she won't..." He stopped to look down at the bear's smiling face, before taking it up to his chest to hold closer to his heart. "You know what I mean, don't you, squirt?" he cried, while reaching out a free hand to touch a finger to her tear-dampened cheek.

"Yes, I do. It's hard to believe she's not going to be here either. Nor, Aunt Catherine."

"Morgan," Steve interrupted, "shall we get this loaded?"

"Yeah, coming. Christy?" he turned.

"Yes?"

"Put this in my carry-on bag, so I can keep it close by."

"Sure, I'll be glad to."

After they had gotten through, Steve and the others took him to the Myrtle Beach Airport, where he met up with Nate, who couldn't look happier, knowing they would all soon be together again.

"Are we ready?" he asked.

"Yeah, just let me double check on the caskets, and get my things on board."

"Morgan, go ahead," Christy motioned with a nod of her head, "we'll get your things here all taken care of."

"Sure?" he asked, looking down at all that he had brought.

"Go," Steve insisted. "We'll be fine here."

Taking that moment, he was off to see the airport manager, and soon he had his answer, while seeing for himself that they were on board, all right.

"Thanks. The last thing I would want is for something horrible to happen to them."

"No one would, Sir!" the stout man, in his late fifties, exclaimed thoughtfully.

With a shake of their hands, Morgan was off to join the others, just as the announcer called out their flight over the intercom.

"Where is he?" Steve asked, as he began to worry.

"He will be here soon. He isn't about to miss this flight," Christy replied, just as they saw him running up the long hallway to get to them.

"Damn, where has the time gone?" he complained, while giving them each a hug goodbye. "We will be seeing you in a few short weeks, right?"

"Count on it, friend," Steve groaned. *Count on it*, he sadly repeated to himself, as Morgan and Nate turned to head down the ramp way to get to their plane.

"Bye...!" they all called out.

Once the door closed, Steve and his family went over to the large plate glass windows to watch as the large craft began taxing down the runway.

"I'm going to miss him," Lacy cried tearfully, as her mother brushed back her daughter's long brown hair from out of her face.

"Yes, but the time will go fast, you'll see," she smiled, while all along her husband stood by quietly.

'*Lord, I know you can hear me. Please watch over our friend, and keep him safe!*' he prayed.

Not taking nearly as long as they thought, their flight landed just outside of New Orleans, where the air was fresh and warm, as the sun was just nearing the horizon at the end of the day.

"What do you say, we get everything all taken care of here, and then head on over to my place?" Nate asked, tiredly.

"Sure. First, I think that's the Hearse, now, here to take them over to the park. After I see to the loading, we will get my other things rounded up, before I go over and see to the plot, to make sure of its location."

"Sure."

Knowing how delicate things like this could be, Nate offered as much help and support that he could, while seeing the tension build throughout his friends' face at seeing his wife's casket being loaded into the back of the first Hearse.

"Nate?" he turned back worriedly.

"Go. I'll get things here all taken care of, and meet you there."

"You know where my things are?"

"Yes. Now hurry!"

Running out to the tarmac, Morgan flagged down the driver of the second Hearse.

"Mr. Fairbanks, I gather?" the well-dressed man, in his fifties, asked. "Mr. Brice has told me to let you know we have one of our own limos here to take you along, so you can see personally to your family's needs."

"Thank you," he replied, while being shown to the car. Stopping though, he saw his little girl's casket being brought out next. "Wait!" he ordered, as he went up to it.

"Sir?" the young man in black jeans and a nicely tailored shirt asked, but then seeing his boss wave him aside, he backed away, as Morgan stepped forward.

"I wish to carry my daughter's casket to the Hearse myself, please."

"Of course, Sir," he bowed his head along with everyone else there, as well as a few workers and passer-byer's that saw the infant's casket.

Once loaded, though, they were off to the cemetery, where by the following morning, he would have the time to himself to see to their burial.

Later that night, not able to sleep, he got up to go out onto the front porch of Nate's five-bedroom house, where he could faintly hear partying off in the distance.

"You hear it too?" Nate asked, having already been sitting out there with a lit cigarette in hand.

"Yeah, but that's not what got me up."

"The burial tomorrow?"

"That too!"

"What else?"

"This plantation. Ted says that it has three stables, but only two are used. Just how much ground are we talking here to have three stables?"

"Would you believe a whopping three hundred acres?"

"At this point, I don't know what to believe. Then, there's this man, Jason was warning me about."

"Copeland? Yeah. Not only have I run into him on a few occasions, but Ramsey, too, had told me about him. That's one more reason why I need you here."

"Why?"

"The stables out at the old plantation."

"What about them?"

"Can we use one to hide a couple of our client's thoroughbreds in?"

"Well, first, before I agree to anything, I need to have a look around the place."

"How about tomorrow, right after you're through?"

Shaking his head, "You sure know how to hurry things along, don't you?"

"Sorry, I wasn't trying to sound unfeeling. I know that. The time with her means a lot to you. It's just that..."

"I know," he sighed heavily. "Tomorrow is fine. Just where is this place anyway?"

"Just the other side of town, about seven or eight miles out."

"Great, if I wanted to be alone, that'll do it."

"Well, you could always get Steve and the others to join you!"

"And have a possible ghost run them out? Not bloody likely," he roared out laughing.

"Yeah, I guess you have a point there," he shook his head, amusingly, before getting up to put out his cigarette.

"Hey, what's wrong with putting them up here?"

"I already arranged that," he laughed, seeing his friends' amused look just then.

"Great, make me feel like the bad guy."

"Sure, why not? After all, who was it that just had to go and fall in love first, before taking that job offer up in Cool Water?"

"Yeah, well you could have joined us!"

"What, and miss all this? Not a chance, buddy."

"Oh, well, it's late, and I need to be getting in touch with that law firm first thing in the morning, if you are wanting me to see the old plantation tomorrow."

"Yes, and besides, I am pretty beat, as well. So I'll see ya in the morning."

"Hey, Nate?" Morgan called out, as his friend reached for the door.

"Yeah?"

"Did you ever find the right gal to settle down with?"

"Me...? Are you kidding?"

"No, huh?" he laughed once more, as he went back inside with his friend.

Chapter Six

By the next morning, the day promised itself to be nice just for the burial. However, the trip out to the plantation was another story. Meanwhile, waking to the smell of coffee brewing, Morgan begrudgingly rolled out of bed, and into a seated position, before rubbing the sleep from out of his eyes. "Mmmm..." he groaned tiredly, as he went to get up. However, feeling a little disoriented, it finally dawned on him where he was.

"Good morning!" Nate called out from the kitchen table, when he came stumbling in.

"What time is it?" he asked, while trying to make out the clock, on the wall, over the counter.

"It's six am! Didn't you get any sleep?"

"Mmmm... some. I can't believe you get up at this time. You hated it back in college."

"That was then. Now people get up before the birds if they have a clinic to run. Besides, I was up at five, not six. And that, my friend, is my second pot of coffee."

"Mmmm..." he groaned again, going over to take out a cup for himself, "I still have to make that call this morning."

"What time are you going to set it for?"

"What?"

"The meeting with the attorneys?"

"If they can get me in, it will be before the Cemetery."

"And when is that to take place?"

"Eleven-thirty, so that they have sufficient enough time to get things ready."

"Well, you are in luck, the weather for today is going to be on your side."

"Good, that's how she would have wanted it," he said, looking down at his watch, before taking a drink of his coffee.

"Hey, while you're waiting, you can always come with me over to the clinic! You know, to get a feel for things, and all!"

"Yeah, I just might do that, or go mad waiting."

Downing their coffee, they each went off to get ready.

For Morgan, going in to get him a quick shower, he decides to pass on the shaving, and gives the shaving kit a toss back into his overnight bag. "Not today," he grumbled, while pulling out a fresh pair of Levis and a black turtleneck sweater he had planned to wear to the Cemetery. Afterwards, he plopped down on the bed and pulled on a pair of worn cowboy boots to go walking around the old plantation in.

"Ready?" Nate asked, seeing him walking out onto the front porch, with his hair combed out, and a day's growth on his face.

"Yes. What are we going in?"

"See for yourself!" He pointed off toward a black, shinny SUV. "A lot like your own in fact."

Laughing, he went over to have a closer look at it. "Well, if you didn't go and take me seriously."

"Hey, what the hay! You said it would sure come in handy when I would least expect it. And you're right, I can haul small animals in it, and some equipment if I have to go out to care for a fallen horse."

"You did good for yourself, Nate, I will say that much for you, you did real good."

Hearing that, meant a great deal to him, being a few years younger than Morgan. And not having a brother to look up to,

Morgan was just the one to have around. "Thanks," he smiled, tearfully.

Looking back, Morgan went up to give him his usual bear hug. "Yeah, well I sure have missed you too, kid. Now let's get going, before we get running behind?"

"Sure. Just give me a sec." Running back up to the house, Nate grabbed a denim jacket, seeing how it was still a little brisk out. Remembering then the jackets he had gotten for his friends in case they decided to join him, he grabbed Morgan's and headed back out with it.

Hearing him return, Morgan looked back to see what he had. "What on earth...?" he laughed.

"Hey, you're down in my country now. So I went and got you one."

Giving it to him, Morgan proudly slipped it on.

"Wow, great fit," Nate cried, looking it over. "And just like mine too."

"Yes, well what about Steve?"

"His jacket is waiting inside for when he gets here."

"You knew we would come, didn't you?"

"Well, I had hoped, and yes, even prayed real hard you guys wouldn't say no. Damn, what do you think? I have missed you two. You especially."

"We were close, weren't we?"

"Like brothers."

"Yes, well, brother, let's get our butts in gear, and go and see this clinic of yours."

Grinning ear to ear, the two hopped into Nate's Tahoe, with Nate behind the wheel.

However, sometime down the road, they met up with another black SUV, an older model Ford Bronco, and the men in it weren't looking all that friendly, when Nate drove passed them.

Just then, all hell broke loose, when the Bronco peeled out behind them.

"What the hell?" Morgan growled, when turning to see it rear up on their back end.

"Oh, damn..." Nate cried, peering into the rearview mirror, just as the other driver was about to slam into his tail end, "I was hoping they wouldn't come after me quite so soon."

"They? Quite so soon? What the hell are you talking about? Who are these guys?"

"Copeland's goons. It's his way of telling me to back off taking care of Jordan's mare. She..." He looked to his friend, "is the one we need you to hide for us. Or should I say, her off-spring, Jack Daniels."

"Jack, what?"

Before he could get the words out, they took a hit to the rear end.

"Jack Daniels. He's coming up next for the big race this spring. Story has it, old man Copeland had Jack Daniel's dad killed last summer, when he won the trophy up at the Kentucky Derby. And boy was he pissed."

Once again, another hit to the rear end.

"Oh, shit!" Nate yelled, as the other SUV pulled around to their left side. When it did, one of the guys on the passenger side pulled out a high-powered rifle, and aimed it at their front tire.

"Hit the brakes_____!" Morgan yelled, while watching the other driver.

"What_____?"

"Just do it, and hold onto the wheel, in case they succeed in hitting the tire after all."

"Then what?" he asked, doing what he was told.

Soon he found out, as the rifle went off, missing its target.

"Remember how we use to switch drivers in the middle of the road?"

"Yes, but that was going at thirty miles an hour! According to this, we are hitting every bit of eighty," he cried, looking down at the speedometer.

"Yeah, well look up ahead of us."

Seeing how they were now behind the Bronco, Nate still looked baffled. "All right, tell me again, what we are about to do?"

"Switch me places. As in, lay the back of your seat flat, while I do the same. Then I'll slide out of mine, and in behind you. When I'm in position, you slide over into my seat. You got that? Oh, and don't forget to set the cruise control, so we won't have to worry about the pedals, until I get into position."

"Is that it?" he asked, nervously.

"No. Hold on to your teeth," Morgan instructed, as the two began trading seats in a hurry.

Once done, they returned their seats in the upright position, as the other vehicle was just about to move over and try shooting out their tire again.

"Oh, no you don't..." Morgan growled, as he rammed the gear down a notch to pull in behind them. Doing so, he looked to his friend. "You do have full coverage, don't you?"

"Uh, huh!"

"Good."

"Oh, but you should know," Nate pointed out, "the road up ahead takes a hairpin turn to the left pretty soon."

Making a note of that, Morgan eased up on the other guy's bumper. "Now, remember what I said about holding onto your teeth? Well, if I were you, I would be doing it right..." he picked up speed even more, "about..." and more, "Now!" he laughed, as he hit the gas as hard as he could, before hitting the brakes in time to swerve hard to the left.

"Wow!" Nate cried, laughing, while turning to see the other vehicle take the six and a half foot drop pretty hard.

Stopping up ahead, while having a look for himself, Morgan asked, "Are you okay?"

"Yes...!" he continued to laugh.

"Good." Seeing how the others were slowly getting out, though apparently not hurt too bad, he grinned. "So this is just a show of what he's made of, huh? I think I will just call Jason, and see if he would like to join us, as well. He has been wanting to explore his horizon a little more," he laughed, while pulling away to head for the animal clinic on the edge of town.

Getting there, he did just that, and in no time, the two were making plans for Jason's arrival.

"Now remember, you are supposed to be my stable hand, and Nate here, doesn't know me personally, since I had just hired him as my vet."

"Sounds good! As for making any arrests, I talked to my Commander this morning, and he is willing to transfer me to their division, so that it will all be nice and legal-like."

"When can you get here?"

"Will tomorrow be soon enough?"

"Tomorrow is fine. Now you know where to find me?" he asked, having gotten the direction from Nate.

"Yes. And Morgan?"

"Yes?"

"It will be great working with you all."

Laughing, "Same here, buddy. Same here." Getting off the phone, he turned back to his friend, "Well, it's all set. Now to call the lawyer."

"Before you do," Nate began, looking a little troubled.

"What is it?"

"I..." he began, while walking back over to the door, seeing how they still had some time before opening. "I should tell you about all the rest of what has been going on around here."

"Oh, shit. There's more?" he asked, taking a seat on the front desk, while picking up on the scent of dusty animals that were caged up in one of the other rooms.

"The lawyer you are about to see."

"What about him?"

"He's Copeland's son."

"What...?"

"Oh, but he is not like his father. In fact," he laughed, "he really made his dad mad when he pursued the rightful owner of the old plantation."

"Why?"

"It seems that Frank Sr. wanted that place for himself. Oh, yes, and get this, the man's grandfather worked for the Captain Morgan, years later though. In fact, I think he's the one who did Michael Fairington in."

"Michael, who?"

"Cynthia's Morgan's lover?"

"Yes, the ghost."

"We don't know that for sure. It has been years since she had been heard from."

"Great."

"But it's true!"

"Listen, about Copeland, I am willing to go along with that, but…"

"I know, not when it comes to ghosts," he laughed, while his friend went on to call the lawyer. *Oh, but you will find out for yourself. When you do, you will be calling on me to get in touch with the psychic,* he smiled, assuredly.

Right after getting off the phone, Morgan turned back to his friend, who was just about to open the doors for business. "You mind if I use the Tahoe?"

"Sure," he replied, tossing him the keys. "Just be careful, they know my vehicle."

"Well, if they don't want a repeat of what happened earlier, they had best stay out of my way," he laughed, walking out, to see Frank Jr.

Chapter Seven

Arriving just outside one of the most elaborate office buildings in the city, Morgan found a spot close by to park. While getting out, he looked around for signs of anything looking the slightest bit suspicious. What he saw though was a half dozen varieties of cars and trucks parked on both sides of the street. None of which looked suspicious. On the other hand, directly across from office was a limo, with its driver standing at the back door, as if waiting on its passenger to return.

From there, he looked off passed the limo, near the entrance of the city park. "Great, just what I needed," Morgan grumbled to himself, seeing what looked to be an old native Indian, wearing a worn dirty white tattered cowboy hat, watching him closely. "Is he one of Copeland's goons, too, or just a..." he started, but before he could finish, a rather tall, large man in his mid-sixties, came barreling out of the office building, like he was on fire.

"That son of a..." he was saying, when slamming into Morgan's own large frame. "Out of my way," he demanded, without really looking at him.

Getting a close enough look to see the man was extremely hot about something, Morgan returned equally hot, "No. Pardon me!"

Not paying him any mind, the man stormed across the street and got into the back seat of the limo, and soon left. As for the onlooker, he continued to watch Morgan, until it was apparent that Morgan was watching him too.

"Just who are you, anyway?" Morgan continued to wonder to himself, as the man then bowed his head and walked away. "What the hell…? Enough of this," he shook his head. "I've got to get this meeting over with, so I can get out to the Cemetery."

Turning, he went on inside, where he was greeted by a warm, friendly brunette, who looked to be in her late twenties, got up to ask, "May I help you?"

"Mr. Fairbanks to see Mr. Copeland."

"That'll be Mr. Copeland Jr., I presume?"

"Yes," Morgan smiled.

"Good. You had just missed Copeland Sr.," she blushed.

"Was that him, just now, barreling out of here?"

"Oh, so you saw him?"

"Saw him? He ran right into me."

"Sorry about that," came a younger version of the man who had just stormed out of there minutes ago, only smiling, as he walked out of his office, while extending a hand out to Morgan. "My father isn't a very happy man these days," he offered in his father's place. "Please, come into my office and we will go over the paperwork on the old estate. Afterwhich, I will take you out to show you the place."

"Am I to understand that your great grandfather worked there years ago for the Captain?"

"No. That would have been my second or third great grandfather, I believe."

"I see."

Meanwhile, going on into the large, well-decorated office, the two took their seats and began going over the legal papers surrounding the estate.

"When your friend called, I was ecstatic to hear there was someone out there still connected to the property. But then, I had to be absolutely sure there could be no mistaking it."

"And you are certain?"

"Oh, yes. The library holds all the records dating back to your late wife's great-great-great-great grandmother's birth. And from what I've found, there's something I think you ought to see."

Taking that moment, he got up to go over to his safe, and soon had it open and a rather large yellow envelope in his hand.

"What is it?" Morgan asked, when it was handed to him.

"A rather interesting piece of your wife's past. I think you ought to read. Your friend tells me, you have no idea what had been causing the women in her family to die, while giving birth. And Morgan. May I call you Morgan?"

"Yes. Yes, of course."

"Pay particular close attention to the part about *little girls*."

"As in what we were to have?"

"Yes."

"I gather you have already been through this?" Morgan asked, looking from the envelope to the Lawyer.

"Oh, for sure."

"Then don't waste my time. Tell me what I need to know."

"Take my word for it, you will want to read it for yourself. As for the legal ins and outs surrounding the Estate. All property taxes have been paid through a trust fund, set up years ago, by Captain Morgan, before his death. Though at the time, his granddaughter came to live there, but only briefly, when she passed, as well, giving birth to a little girl."

"Was she married at that time?" Morgan asked puzzledly.

"Yes."

"Then why didn't it go to her husband?"

"Take a look in your paperwork I gave you. It clearly states that the Estate remains in the family. That, and after the

Captain's death, the husband thought the Estate was haunted. So he ran out of there, leaving everything that belonged to it behind. Later a caregiver came along and covered everything, and then continued to see to the grounds so the place wouldn't get too run down."

"I'm glad to hear that! Did he get paid for doing all that?"

"Yes, from the same trust fund."

Shaking his head, Morgan was still bothered by something he had said.

Seeing this, Frank Jr. asked, "What is it? You look as though something doesn't add up."

"This whole family thing. If it had have not been for my late wife, there would have been no more left to pass it to. And like you said, it would have had to have been sold."

"Actually, auctioned off. And my father would have seen to it no one topped his bid. So now, how about we take these papers with us, and talk more out there. I don't really trust the ears around here."

"On account of your father?" Morgan grinned.

"Yes, he has more people on his payroll than you can imagine."

"But not you?"

"No, and that's what has him so furious."

"Then I can trust you?"

"Count on it," he returned, while reaching for his jacket.

On their way out, Frank led the way to one of the few pickups, out front, that belonged to him.

"Why don't I just follow you," Morgan suggested, while heading over to Nate's Tahoe.

"Is that yours?" he asked, looking puzzled at the shiny black SUV.

"No. It belongs to that friend of mine. Why?"

"My father's men know it. And if they see it out..."

"You don't have to tell me. We met with them earlier," he repeated his grin.

"Oh?"

Laughing, "Yes, and they didn't seem all that happy either, when windup up in a six and a half foot drainage ditch."

Laughing, too, he shook his head. "That, by any chance, wasn't you behind the wheel, was it?"

"Not at first," he continued to grin, while going on over to open the driver's side door.

"I don't know though. They may have had a taste of their own medicine, but they don't give up so easy. My father would see to that."

"Well, let them just try," he growled. *'Let them just try.'*

Getting in, the two were off, heading for the south side of town. So far, there hadn't been any signs of Frank Senior's men anywhere.

"Good," Morgan noted to himself, while keeping his guard up.

Not long after, he saw the old Morgan Plantation coming up on the right, as Frank signal

ed he was about to turn in. But then, out of nowhere, came another black Bronco with the same men in it from before.

Slowing down just as Morgan was about to make his own turn, he stopped precisely at the side of it, and glared at them. "Boys," he growled, "let's be smart, won't we, and not miss with me. You won't like it one bit if I have to teach you another lesson on your driving abilities."

"So, that piece of fine work was your doing, huh?" the husky man, looking to be in his late thirties, with brown hair and blue eyes, grinned from behind the wheel.

"Sure was!" he grinned back. "Liked it, did you?"

"Hmmm... we will just have to see what else you can do now, won't we?"

"Is that an invitation to trouble, I hear?"

"Oh, no, not at all! Actually, I had thought that this SUV was someone else's."

"Meaning?"

"Well, if we startled you, let me just say, I'm sorry for the mistaken identity. It won't happen again."

Yeah, I just bet it won't, he growled. "Well, let me enlighten you some. I don't tolerate being bullied, while I'm here to settle some business."

"Oh? And what might that be?"

Looking off toward the mansion, with its straggly vines growing up the sides of the grand walls, and its wraparound veranda, not far off the road, he turned back, seeing how they too, looked off at the place. "Do I have to spell it out?"

"That's yours? You're the rightful owner?"

"My late wife was. Now it is mine to carry on in her memory. And if I so much as feel your presence around here..." He dropped the rest for them to figure out.

"Your... late... wife...?" he asked, puzzledly.

"Catherine Habersham-Fairbanks." At that, he smiled, and nodded his adieu, before pulling away.

"Damn," one of the other men, a young swanky looking one in the back seat gulped, "Mr. C. isn't going to like this."

"Whose going to tell him?" the driver asked, thinking back on what Morgan had said about his late wife, not to mention, the Habersham name.

"Jarred, he wants this place for himself. You know that," the short stocky-looking guy in the front seat groaned.

"Yeah, well we will just have to think of some other way of getting it. As for now, not a word out of any of you. You got that?" he threatened, while looking into the rearview mirror at the two in the backseat.

"Yeah, whatever you say," the fourth, though being the closest to the driver as friends get, replied, while picking up on something in the way he was watching the Tahoe move farther off in the distance.

Pulling away, Jarred headed back to the Circle C Ranch, where after dropping them off, he was about to leave, when his friend turned back to see he wasn't sticking around.

Calling out stopping him, the lanky, light-brown haired guy in his early thirties ran up to see where he was going. "Wait up, buddy. Where you off to in such a hurry?"

"Just out," he announce gruffly.

"Good." Opening the front passenger side door, he got in. "How about I just go with you? I wanted to talk to you anyway."

"What about?"

"The look that came over you, when that guy mentioned his late wife."

"What's to talk about?" he asked, pulling away.

"You knew her, did you?"

"Yes, you could say that."

"Did you also know she was the rightful heiress to the old plantation?"

"No. God no..." he fought hard to keep from breaking down. "Damn it, Scott, she was my sister's best friend, back in high school."

"Oh, hell no. Now what?"

"What do you mean?"

"Mr. C, he trusts us to tell him everything."

"I'm not telling him a damn thing."

"Then what..."

"Oh, damn...!" he groaned, cutting him off, when seeing their boss head their way. Looking sharply to his friend, he growled, "Remember what I said earlier? Not a damn word. Just let me handle him my own way."

"Sure. You can trust me not to say a word." He clammed up and turned to look away.

"Yes, but what of the others?" he asked hurriedly, before their boss pulled up alongside them. "They don't know what you now know."

Turning back to study him, "No, but you'll talk to them. They'll keep their mouths shut, or you will beat them to death if they open them."

Grinning, Scott knew his friend's temperament, but before anything more could be said, Copeland pulled to a stop, and rolled his window down. "Anything yet?" he asked, bitterly.

"No," Jarred growled, while looking directly into the man's old weather-beaten face.

"Damn him, he just had to go against me and locate that son of a..." he stopped for a moment to think back on the man he had run into outside his son's office.

"What?" Jarred asked, nonchalantly.

"Earlier, at Frank's office, I had just came out angrier than all get out, when I slammed right into this man."

"Oh?" the two replied at the same time, while looking to each other, knowingly.

"Yes... Listen up, I want the two of you to high tail it out to the old plantation, and see if you see anyone. Then get back to me as soon as you know anything."

"Sure, we'll get right on it," Jarred returned, knowing things weren't going to be the same anymore. Once Copeland pulled away, he glared back in his rearview mirror at the man.

"So, what are we going to do now?"

"Not what he wants us to do!" he grinned ominously, and pulled away.

"What then?"

"My sister loved that girl, and Ma did too, since Cathy's mother died giving birth to her. So I'll be damned if he goes and wrecks her memory now."

"You're going against Mr. C?"

"Yeah, just maybe, and if I do, are you going to turn on me?"

"Jarred, we've been buddies for a hell of a long time, and you know how I feel about your sister."

"Yeah, and I know how she's so dumbfounded crazy over you. So, I'll ask you once
more..."

"No. I'm..." he gritted his teeth at the price they would surely pay once they had been founded out. "I'm with you, all the way."

"Good. Now let's go out and see Cathy's man. I want to get to know who my little adopted sister went on to marry without telling us about him."

Meanwhile, back at the old plantation, Frank went on to tell about how he and his father went their separate ways. "It all started when my mom was sick. Dad had been getting more and more involved with the horse races, and not caring about what was taking place at home. Soon, she was rushed off to the hospital, where they couldn't save her. I was so full of bitterness by then toward him. If I had half the balls he does, I would have killed him myself."

"And now?"

"We just tolerate each other."

"If your father was to, say, put out a hit on someone's thoroughbred, would you tell me? And or would you tell me if he were to try and hurt someone?"

"If I were to hear of it, yes."

"Good. For now, I have seen enough. So I have got to go and see about my late wife's burial."

"All right. Oh, and by the way, just where are you staying?"

"Nate's place, until I get this one fixed back up."

"Does this mean you will be starting up your practice here?"

"No, that will be our friend and his wife, Christy," he laughed.

"Oh, what is so funny?" Frank Jr. asked.

"I'm leaving my practice to become a Veterinarian. As it seems, Nate needs some help."

"Good. Old Doc Ramsey has spoke highly of him. Just tell him to watch his back, won't you?"

"Oh, but he knows that already. In fact, just before turning into the drive, I met some of your father's boys."

"Oh?"

"Yes. And yes, we had our little talk about messing with the wrong man."

"I'm sure they liked that. Especially Jarred, he is one of dad's number one men, next to Bart, that is."

"Jarred, huh?"

"Yes, you know him? Oh, but how could you? You had only gotten here just the other day!"

"You're right, but it sure seems that I should know that name."

"Maybe it will come to you later, after you have had some time to settle in."

"Yes, just maybe."

"Well, I should be going. I have court tomorrow, and I need to get ready for it."

"Yes, and I have to get going myself."

Before getting back into their vehicles, Morgan stopped the man.

"One question though."

"Yes?"

"Your father. Aside from you, I have heard a lot about him."

"Oh, I'm sure you have!" he grinned. "And no doubt you will be hearing more. What's your question?"

"Well seeing how your relationship is with him. And though it isn't any of my business, but when he passes away, who gets his place?" he laughed to keep the subject at hand upbeat.

Laughing, as well, he returned, "That's just one of the things about being an Attorney."

"Oh?"

"I did up his Will, and made certain it would be left to me and not his henchman, Bart, as he so wanted it to be, when we got into our huge fight over my mother."

"Let me guess, he cut you out of it?"

"Yes. Oh, but I told him that was fine in order to get him to trust me enough to let me draw up the new one."

"And in the new one you would have been able to…"

"Reword it enough to make it look as though Bart was mentioned. Oh, but don't get me wrong," he chuckled, "*he* was mentioned. Providing that he takes the family business straight.

And too, upon his own death, everything dad left him would revert back to me."

"Smart. It's nice to see you truly aren't your father's son after all."

"No, I am one hundred percent my mother's son, and always will be. I hate that son of a…" He stopped to reframe from going on.

With that, the two grinned admiringly, and left, heading back into town, where Morgan made a quick pit stop at the clinic, to check on his friend.

Walking in, right away he spotted the old Indiana, in the dirty white cowboy hat, drinking coffee, while carrying on what seemed to be a friendly conversation with Nate, who was busying himself with a sick German Sheppard.

"Nate…?" Morgan spoke up, curiously, while closing the door behind him.

"Hey there, you're back! Is everything all right with the Tahoe? And were you able to get out to see the old plantation all right?"

"Yes, your Tahoe is just fine, and the old plantation, no doubt needs some work. Now, what the hell is going on here?" he glared, now getting a closer look at the old man standing in front of him. "Indian, I take it?" he asked abruptly.

"Morgan…"

"No, that's quite all right," the man said, smiling. "You must be wondering what I was doing, watching you so close back in town."

"Well, the thought had crossed my mind!"

"You know each other?" Nate stopped to ask puzzledly.

"No," the man replied. "After your telling me of his arrival, I took it upon myself to keep an eye on him."

"Why?" Morgan growled.

"Morgan," Nate interjected, "this is Chief Ramsey. The…"

"Ahhh… the retired doctor, or I should say, vet.," he replied, offering an apology for his rudeness. "I'm terribly sorry. He didn't tell me…"

"That I was an old Indian?" he grinned.

"No."

"That's quite all right. And now, how was your visit with young Franklin?"

"Good! He filled me in on his wrath was his father. It looks as though we will have at least one good ally on our side."

"No," came the sound of a man, walking in just then.

Chapter Eight

Turning, everyone saw Jarred and his friend, Scott, walk in, closing the door behind them.

"You again," Morgan glared, heatedly.

"Yes, but I'm not here to cause anyone any trouble."

"Then what are you here for? A sick or injured animal?" Nate asked, bravely. "Or perhaps to put your boss out of his misery?"

Laughing, he shook his head. "No, I'm here to see my sister's husband."

"What?" the two asked, looking around them.

"Who?" Nate asked.

"Him," he smiled boldly at Morgan.

"Me?"

"Yes, Cathy was my adopted sister. Or to make it easier on you, she was my little sister's best friend in high school, before she just had to go off to college up in West Virginia."

"Wait a minute, now I remember that name. Frank mentioned it earlier. You're Jarred Ashford, and your sister..."

"Brenda Ashford," he replied, grinningly. "Your wife was loved very deeply by us all, including my mother and father. As it was, they had taken her in under their wing, when the two had met. That's after learning of her mother's death. Even her father was a great man in his years, but the guy couldn't stand the loss of his wife any longer, when his own health started to plummet. It was awful to see him go just before her graduation."

"So she told me. Now it's kinda funny, though, getting back to realizing who you are."

"How's that?"

"We came down to see you and your family last year, but you all had gone somewhere. Something to do with a death in the family," he offered sadly.

"My father. He had had a few too many strokes. The last one took him."

"Sorry to hear that. Meanwhile, back to when the two of you walked in. You said '*no.*' What were you referring to?"

"Your one ally. You have two more now."

"How can I trust you, when you work for Copeland?"

"You will just have to try."

"And you?" Morgan turned to the other man, who all that time remained quiet.

"Jarred and I have been close friends for a real long time. That, and if," he turned to his buddy, grinning, "I am going to marry his sister, I had better know which side to stand on."

"Damn straight," he growled.

"I wish I could just say yes, but I can't. Not until I have had sufficient enough time to get to know the two of you. As for you, Jarred, Cat has told me how trusting you can be. Then there is the matter to get settled about this morning's incident."

"We were only following orders," Scott offered, apologetically.

"Yes, and are you going to continue to follow his orders?"

Both men looked to each other bitterly.

"No. At least not directly," Jarred replied.

"Meaning?"

"To steer clear of his wrath, we're going to let him assume that we are," he explained. "Though, I can't speak for the others."

"Then we will just have to come up with something. However, I must be going, I still have to get out to the Cemetery, before it gets to being too much later."

"The Cemetery?" Jarred asked, puzzledly.

"Cat's burial, along with our little girl."

"You..." He stopped. "Oh, Christ, it did happen again, didn't it?"

"Yes, and I am about to find out why, just as soon as I get things settled, that is."

"Mom and Brenda would want to know. But then, you might want it to be private."

"I would prefer it to be that way, but knowing Cat the way I do, she would have wanted them to be there. So, by all means, call them. It's to take place..." He looked down at his watch, "Damn... right about now!"

Taking out his cell phone, Jarred quickly dialed his mother's house, where he knew his sister would be.

Filling them in, his sister asked, "Are you going to be there?"

"Bren, you know if Mr. C. saw me there, he would no doubt get suspicious."

"I don't see why you just don't leave that job. You and Scott both. He is bad news."

"Come on, sis, you know why I don't leave him. We need the money, too, bad."

Hearing this, gave Morgan an idea, as he turned to the others. Filling them in, they

nodded their agreement in silence, just as Jarred was about to get off the phone.

"I'll ask him, but for now tell mom to hurry. It's supposed to be going down now."

"But how will we know where to go, once we get there?"

Turning to Morgan, he asked.

"Its along with the rest of the family of Habersham's. Just look for the family plot, with its white rod iron fence around it. It's along Marc Twains Lane."

"Did you hear that?" he asked his sister.

"Yes, and make sure you tell him who has been taking care of it all this time."

"I will." Getting off the phone, he tucked it back inside his vest pocket. "She wanted you to know who had been caring for the plot all this time."

"I know. The park manager filled me in. Thanks."

"Hey, you guys," Scott spoke up, while looking out the front window, "if we're done with this warm reunion!"

"Do we have a problem?" Jarred asked, going over to the window.

"No, not yet, but just the same, we need to be cutting this a bit short."

"Where are you parked?" Morgan asked right away.

"Out back, where it's the safest," Jarred returned, joining them.

"Good. In that case," Turning to his friend, "can they go on out the back door?"

"Sure!" Nate agreed. "I'll just take you there, myself!"

"Nate," Morgan called out, "I'm heading on out, as well."

"See you back at the house later?"

"Not if I come back here first."

Saying their goodbyes, everyone but Ramsey and Nate went their own way.

Reaching the Cemetery, Morgan went right to the family plot, carrying two very large arrangements, one for each of the sites.

"Mr. Fairbanks!" Norman Brice greeted him warmly.

"Mr. Brice!"

"Would you like for me to take those for you?" he asked, coming forward in his black tailored suit to offer a hand.

"No, that'll be all right, I have them!"

"Of course," he bowed his head in respect. "I have also took the liberty of bringing with me a CD player, and a wide selection of lovely music, if you would like to pick through them."

After placing the flowers over the tops of each casket, he stood quietly for a moment.

"Sir?"

"I'm sorry, you were saying?"

"The music. I took the liberty of bringing a CD player with a wide selection of music."

"Oh, of course."

"Would you like to see what I have? Perhaps it will help soothe things along for you."

"Again I'm sorry, but I can't think of music at this time. So please..." He waved a hand in the air in sadness.

"Perhaps I can help!" a young woman near his late wife's age, spoke up, just as she and her mother walked up to join him.

Turning, he saw a younger image of Jarred standing next to a woman with graying hair, and the prettiest of blue eyes he had ever seen, aside from his wife's. "Mrs. Ashford, I gather?"

"Yes, and my..."

"Brenda," he smiled softly.

Seeing his smile, as well as his own warm and gentle eyes, a tear ran down her cheek. "I can see now why Cathy married you," she replied in kind.

"Oh?"

"Your eyes, and of course that smile. She said that would be the ticket to true and everlasting love. One that would carry on forever."

"And she was right! As it was her eyes that caught me the instant I bumped into her, just outside the campus coffee shop!"

"She said something about meeting someone, but after that, we had lost touch with each other. I guess this would mean that you are to blame for that," she teased.

"Guilty as charged. But I should tell the two of you, we came down to see you last summer, in hopes to make up for all the lost time."

"My husband," Mary sadly spoke up, "had passed away then."

"Yes, Jarred told me. I'm terribly sorry to hear that. I heard as well that your family sort of took Cat in, knowing of her mother's passing, and all."

"Yes. Her father wasn't doing much better, either."

"So I have been told."

"In fact..."

Seeing how Brenda was fishing for whether or not to call him by his first name, or not, he smiled again. "Its Morgan, Miss Ashford. Please, call me Morgan."

"M...Morgan...?"she cried. "Oh, my, gosh... she said she would meet a Morgan someday. Just like the plantation."

"Oh? She never told me that!" he mused at first, when something else struck him. It was something in the way Frank had insisted that he ought to read about his wife's past for himself. *'Take my word for it,'* he insisted, *'you would want to read it for yourself. And Morgan,'* he went on, *'pay particular attention to the part about 'little girls.'*

"Morgan...? Morgan, what is it?" the two were asking, while the manager was flipping through the arrangements of CD's.

"Something the lawyer said, concerning Cat's family."

"What was it?" Mary asked, while Brenda stood silent, feeling she already knew.

"It was some information in a packet he gave me. Something to do with information on her past, dating way back."

"Oh, my!" Brenda cried, when finally coming forward about it. "I think I know...!"

"Sweetie," Her mother turned, "does this have anything to do with what the two of you were doing at the library that day, back in high school?"

"Yes," she said, turning back to Morgan, "we were just messing around, talking to some of the guys, and out of nowhere, came this woman."

"Woman?" Morgan prompted.

"Yes. She looked kinda funny. Her clothes were, well, she looked like a gypsy."

"Oh, I bet I know who you are referring to," Mary replied, seeing Morgan's puzzled expression. "She's the town's psychic."

"Great, more paranormal balderdash."

"Oh, but no...!" Brenda cried. "It's true! She pointed right at Cathy and told her she was

going to die, just like her mother, and her mother's mother, and..."

"Brenda... Stop that!" her mother scolded.

"No, I want to hear more, just not right now," he replied, seeing how Mr. Brice was waiting, patiently, yet he had a look of interest written on his face at what was just said. "I'm sorry, you're probably wanting to get on with this, while having other things to do."

"No, my schedule is pretty much cleared, until later this afternoon. So please, if any of you have some music you wish for me to play, tell me now so I can put it on."

"Yes, I do!" Brenda announced, while coming forward to hand him one of hers and Cat's favorite songs. "We used to sing to this all the time. Remember mom?" she turned to ask, with tears streaming down her cheeks.

"Yes, and sing... you would think those two had a voice of an angel coming down from the heavens, Mr.... I mean, Morgan," she blushed.

"In that case, please, enlighten me," he bowed, as Brice set the CD in motion.

Soon, the air was filled with the most heavenly of all sounds, as she sang with all her heart, when then it began to break at the thought of having lost her best friend.

Even then, listening to it, Morgan's own handsome face broke down into tears, when it began to sound as though his own beloved Catherine was standing right next to him, singing. Looking to the heavens, he cried as he had never cried before. When he did, a fine mist of rain came down over him.

Soon the song ended, when Mary and Brenda turned to see his tears of pain streaming down his broken face.

"Morgan..." Brenda too cried, as she went over to offer her sympathies.

"Thanks for sharing that with me," he uttered out sadly, as the two stood holding each other.

Soon though, their moment of peace was shattered, when a black limo pulled up, and the driver, the same as earlier, got out to open the back door.

"Damn, him..." Morgan thundered beneath his breath, "What on earth is he doing here?"

Chapter Nine

Pulling away slightly, Brenda looked up to see a strong hint of anger written on Morgan's face. "You know him too?" she asked, with a hint of surprise in her voice.

"Know him? Only through a friend of mine back home, as well as his own son, and now of course your brother."

"Mr. Fairbanks," Frank Sr. called out, while walking on up, as his driver went around to the other side of the car to take out a most beautiful arrangement of flowers, both for his wife and their little girls' gravesites. "I just came out to offer my condolences, as well as to say I'm sorry for this morning's run in. So please," he turned to his driver, as the tall masculine man looking to be in his forties approached them, "accept these beauties as a peace offering, won't you?"

"I'll show you peace offering," Brenda muttered under her breath, though her comment did not go without notice, when Morgan and Copeland turned to look at her.

"Ah... Miss Brenda, and of course, Ms. Mary. How lovely to see the two of you. Why you both look absolutely lovely today."

"Stuff it, Copeland," Brenda growled, as she was about to step forward, when Morgan stepped around to stop her.

"Mr. Copeland, I presume?" Morgan said, putting on a front, while acting as though he had never heard of him.

"Yes. I believe you have already met my boy earlier?"

"Yes, and he is quite a man," he corrected almost bitterly.

"Well, I didn't really come out here to talk about my son. I just wanted to welcome you to our fair city, and hope that your visit is a nice one."

"My visit?" he questioned grinningly. "Don't you mean my stay?"

"Y...your..."

"Stay. Oh, yes, Mr. Copeland, I'm staying. In fact, I do believe you know the place. It's referred as the old Morgan's Plantation. I even heard that you were wanting it for yourself!" he began to cut loose on his building anger, when Mary and Brice stepped forward, to remind him of why he was there.

Seeing their looks of concern, he swallowed hard on his bitterness, and just turned away.

"Well, for your information, yes, I do..." he slipped up, catching himself, although a bit too late. Morgan turned back sharply, with eyes of icy hot venom, glared directly at the man.

Seeing this, the driver stepped forward, feeling Morgan's move was meant to attack his boss.

"Bart, that won't be necessary. I'm sure Mr. Fairbanks is just upset over the loss of his wife and child."

"Damn straight, I am! And furthermore, this is a private viewing, how *dare* you come uninvited to this burial."

"Yes, of course, I should have exercised a little compassion, and waited until a more opportune time to see you."

"A more opportune time...?" he growled, taking a threatening step forward, with both fists clenched tightly at his sides. Then, turning to see the look on Bart's stony face, he glared even more at him. "If you were smart, you would take your boss home."

"Oh, but when he is ready, Sir," he bowed insultively, while glaring back just as venomously. "When he's ready."

"Oh, but he is," he corrected, warningly, and with a look to put all to shame.

"Now, gentlemen!" Brice came forward, as no one there noticed a black Bronco off in the distance. How long it had been there, was anyone's guess.

Meanwhile, sitting just out of sight, but enough to see what was going on, Jarred could pick up bits and pieces of their heated conversation. "Great, I just might have to show which side I'm on if this blows up anytime soon."

"Maybe not," Scott spoke up, just as Brenda peered over Morgan's tall frame to see them standing there. Signaling for her to keep silent, he smiled amusingly.

"What?" Jarred asked, seeing his sister look off toward his mother.

"Just watch."

And watch they did, when soon, Copeland and his driver, as well as strong arm, pulled back to return to the limo.

"I'm terribly sorry, Mr. Fairbanks, but this wasn't to have turned into a brawl. Please, accept the flowers as my humble apology, and with any hopes, we will talk again later, on how you are getting on with your new living arrangements. However," Copeland stopped to look back, "if you were to decide to sell the old Plantation, you just might like what I have to offer you on the place."

"Somehow, Copeland, I kind of doubt it," he glared.

"Well, just the same, think about it. It would be in your best interests."

"Oh? Now that wouldn't be a threat I hear, would it?"

"No," the man returned. "Just a mere insight of what could happen if you were to sell it to anyone else," Copeland smiled, with a note of underlying sarcasm in it.

Seeing Copeland heading out, Jarred and Scott stood quietly, until the coast was clear, before making their presence known.

"I am terribly sorry, Sir," Brice spoke up, while looking pretty shaken, "but he can be pretty persuasive, if you know what I mean."

"So I hear."

"Morgan, you're not alone," Brenda pointed.

"What..." he started, when turning to see what she was referring to.

Seeing for himself, Jarred and Scott came walking toward them, smiling. "Well, and just how long were you two standing out there?" he grinned.

"Long enough," Jarred returned, while going up to give his mother a big hug.

"Brenda," Scott took his lady to hold. "Thanks for not giving us away back there."

"You knew they were there?" Morgan asked.

"No, not at first, but then something caught my eye," she smiled up at her love.

"Well, enough of this, I need to be getting back to Nate's clinic, just in case one of Copeland's men decide to pay him another visit."

"Oh, but he did," Jarred laughed.

"What...?"

"He's okay!" Scott added grinningly. "We set it up to look like he was being harassed."

"And how was that?"

"When Copeland called to order us to make another hit..." Jarred began.

"We in turn called Nate to fill him in on what was to go down!" Scott finished, smiling.

"And how did he take it?"

"Like a real trooper!" Jarred laughed. "The whole thing was played out really well. After our call, he told his clients that he had an emergency out of the office."

"And as soon as they cleared the place," Scott went on, "we moved in and started breaking out a few windows that Jarred, here, had agreed to replace himself!"

"Jarred!" his mother cried.

"It's all right, Ma. No one got hurt over it. And just before coming here, we went in through the back door, after ditching the Bronco, to see how they were!"

"They?" Morgan asked.

"Yes," Scott offered, "Chief Ramsey was there at the time, too."

"Good," Morgan sighed.

"But still, do you have to do his bidding?" she continued.

"Ma, we've been over this time and again! We need the money to pay off dad's medical bills. As it is, Copeland owns most of the other businesses around here. And what he doesn't own, he has stuffed down into his back pocket!"

"Well, he doesn't have me or my friends' clinic," Morgan announced, firmly. "So how about coming to work for one of us?"

"Sure, I can see it now," Scott quivered, "he'll just have us killed, like he did..."

"Scott!" Jarred turned, cutting him off.

"The black stallion?" Morgan guessed correctly. "And what he is planning on doing to the mare and its offspring 'Jack Daniels' if we don't get them hidden?"

"You know about that?" he asked, surprisingly.

"We all do," Brice added, after gathering up his things so that the groundskeepers could wrap up with their work.

"What do you know?" Morgan asked.

"He is about to make a move, and soon if no one does anything about it," he declared.

Shaking his head, Morgan knew what had to be done. "All right."

"What?" Everyone turned puzzledly to see what he had to say.

"Nate came to me the other night, and told me what was happening. Since this is all so new to me, I told him I didn't know until I first had a look around the old place."

"And have you?" Brenda asked, wide eyed.

"I was out there earlier, but… no, I haven't really gotten all that good of a look."

"We have all been out there a time or two," Mary admitted, shamefully.

"Mom…!" Brenda cried.

"Well…!"

"I think over the years, we all have," Brice admitted, as well.

"Even Cat?" Morgan asked, while looking back on her casket.

"Oh, yeah, even that little brat," Jarred laughed, looking upon her casket, as well, when he went over to lay a single white rose on it. "Even, my little brat," he repeated tearfully.

"Yes, but…" Brenda broke off, remembering her friends' reaction to the boarded up stable that was located far off in the back of the property.

"What?" Morgan insisted. "What were you just about to say?"

"It's nothing," she lied. "We were all just out to have some fun, was all."

"Was it?" he glared, knowing by her expression, she was keeping something from him.

Before parting company, he turned back to her, "Miss Brenda," he began, by adapting to the southern ways, "we will talk again. And I want to know more about this supposed psychic and what all she had to say about my wife's family. And Jarred," he turned, "I want to see you back at Nate's clinic to go over an idea that just might make it beneficial for the two of you."

"Sure."

With a nod of their heads, everyone left him to be alone with his wife and daughter a while longer.

Not long after, subsequent to having said his last goodbyes, he was on his way over to see Nate and Jarred. Getting there, as he was about to walk in, he saw a black mysterious truck go slowly by. "Great, our friendly Mr. Copeland. Just when will he take a hint and find somebody else to bother. Damn him!" Shaking it off, he went on in to see Nate working with a sheepdog that had gotten himself tangled in some barbed wire. Not far off were a man and his son, looking on worriedly.

"Will he make it, Doc.?" he asked, while wringing his hands nervously together.

"I'll know... in just... a few more... minutes," Nate groaned, while cutting the last few strands. "Good," he finished, when looking up to see Morgan standing by in case he was needed. "Hey there, I'm glad you're here!"

"Yeah? Well I see how most of the mess was cleaned up, whatcha need?"

"I could use a hand here. As for the mess, our friend came back and swept it up, before rushing off to meet with his mother and sister, so he said."

"Yes, I saw him. How about the window?"

"He'll be back to get that taken care of soon."

"Soon?"

Morgan saw how his friend wasn't really all that happy to talk about it, and dropped it when he looked up at him over a pair of reading glasses to see by.

Smiling, Nate pointed back to a room behind him. "If you really want to help, you will find some antibiotic in a cabinet. Get it for me, will you? And a syringe too," he called out after Morgan walked off to get it. "Fill it to..." he thought, "three cc's. That should help fight off any infection. Oh, and Morgan," he called out again, just as the man and his son looked up at hearing the name, "I will need a vile of tetanus vaccine too."

Bringing them out, he quickly filled the syringe and gave it to his friend.

"Excuse me," the man spoke up, "but did you say, Morgan?"

"Yes, why?" Nate looked up at him puzzledly.

"We were just wondering, is all."

"Wondering what?" Morgan asked, while looking at the man suspiciously.

"The name, as well as the plantation. Well, let me start over," he grinned, sheepishly. "We are new here. Well at least a year or so. My name is Daniel Moore, and this is my son, Gregory. We heard some things about that place, and well, we were just wondering, is all."

"You mean, like ghosts?" Jarred asked, grinningly.

"Yeah, exactly!"

"Mr. Moore, is it?" Morgan spoke up, distastefully. "I don't believe in ghosts, and as to the name! It was left to my late wife, passed down from generation to generation. Unfortunately, she wasn't here to be a part of it for herself."

"I'm sorry to hear that," he offered, solemnly. "However, I should tell you, that it seems that we are your neighbor."

"Oh? That's always good to know," he returned with a silent smirk, while trying his best to be polite.

Finishing up on the man's dog, he paid his bill and gave Nate a five-dollar tip for his kindness, and soon left.

Looking back to see Morgan's not so friendly expression, Nate laughed, "We get all kinds in here. That one is from Indiana. I think he even said Morristown, or something or other."

"Great, a Hoosier," he laughed.

"That's not all," he went on.

"What do you mean?"

"This dog! The Moore's had found it wondering their place over the winter!"

"So?"

"Yeah, well it came from your place."

"Well, it's his now!" he returned, while going over to pour himself a cup of coffee. "Anyway, shall we get on with this plan of mine?" he asked Jarred.

"W...what?" Jarred asked, thinking he had seen a dog like that one before.

"The plan on having you two come and work for me, and still keep both your heads with Copeland."

"Sure!"

Taking a seat on the counter, everyone listened in closely, while he went on with putting the two to work in the stables. However, not once did he mention Jason's name, as to keep him out of the picture for the time being.

Once he was finished, he looked to each one of them, including Ramsey, when he walked back in earlier to listen in.

"Well, what do you think?"

"Sure!" Scott commented.

"I just had another thought though," Jarred spoke up.

"Let's hear it."

"Copeland just might use this to his advantage, too."

"Thinking that you would tell him if anything that was going on around there?" he grinned. "Done thought about it."

"And you trust us, not to say anything?" Scott asked. Seeing the looks that came over their faces, he coward down in a nearby chair, "I guess if I were to value my health."

"You had best keep your mouth shut," Jarred growled.

"Well, if we're at an understanding, I need to go back over to the plantation and see what all I will be needing to get started on fixing it up."

"Want any company?" Jarred asked, willingly.

"Maybe, later. I still have that paperwork to read over on her past."

"Sure. And while you're at it, I'll see what Ma wanted just before we got here."

"Oh?" he asked.

"Yeah, I think she was wanting me to stop over and pick up some food she was wanting to make for you, incase you were to go back out there."

"That sounds awfully nice of her. Tell her thanks." With that he was back out the door, but not before promising to check in with his friend from time to time.

"And Morgan..." Nate called out, knowing how he was going to be without his vehicle.

"If I get done here, I'll see if Ramsey can give me a ride out there."

"Oh, yeah, sure thing," he smiled, when looking back at the Tahoe.

Chapter Ten

Heading out, the drive was smooth and uneventful, no signs of trouble. However, pulling in, Morgan had no idea what was waiting for him inside of this grand old plantation home, when pulling up to the two front doors it had to offer.

Nevertheless, inside, having thought she had been asleep for what seemed like an eternity, the beautiful blonde, with clear-water blue eyes, and an angelic face, got up from her bed to wisp down to the main floor. Before getting there, she stopped at the top of the grand staircase and froze, thinking she had heard someone outside. "Huh, somebody is here!" she smiled, while racing on down to the front doors to meet her visitor. Suddenly, having no time to stop, when the big double doors opened, she cried out, as she slid right through him.

Doing so, it had caused a rush of cold air to hit him, when he stopped to shake it off.

"What...?" she cried, feeling the oddest thing happen to her. "I just passed right through him. But how?" she wondered, frightfully, when she heard him grunt out his disgust.

"Boy, is this what it's like being closed up for over a hundred years?" he grumbled, while going back out on the porch to grab a box of newspapers, before going around back to find some firewood.

Having been told the fireplace was still operable; he wanted to get a fire going to throw off the chill, before getting too late. However, the chill wasn't only due to the house being closed up for so long, but what was looming right in front of him, when returning with the newspapers.

Walking in, he stopped momentarily to close the door.

"Could it be...?" she cried, when surprised at what she had seen in front of her. *"Has he come back for me after all...these..."* Stopping, she looked around the place, and before uttering another word, he took a step forward, coming nose to nose with her. *'Mmmm...'* she noted his breath so warm, and yet fresh with a hint of winter mint on it. *"And his eyes, green as I recalled them to be all those times he had looked into mine. As for his build, so magnificent. But his clothing, what is it about his clothing?"* she asked herself, while looking over his attire. *"It's..."* She touched his sweater, when thinking beneath it she could feel his heart beat. *"Oh, my...!"* she cried, when pulling back quickly at what she felt. *"I don't understand!"* Looking back up into his eyes, she noticed something was missing. Then it started to become clear to her, as if he hadn't even seen her standing there, at all. *"But..."* She stopped again, *"maybe a kiss. That will surely catch his attention."* Giving it a shot, she reached up and kissed the tip of his nose.

Once again, he waved at the air, as if something had just tickled his nose. "Damn, I had better be getting that fire going, before it gets dark. It's cold enough in here, as it is."

"So, you did feel that, did you?" she teased, as he took the box of papers on into what was once the parlor.

Going over to sit them down near an old brown brick fireplace at the far side of the room, he turned to go back out to get him a healthy load of wood.

While he was gone, she went over curiously to look at the papers. At that moment, it hit her, the date at the top read: April 7th, 2002. *"What? But..."* she cried, covering her mouth, *"how could I have been..."* Stopping, she turned, hearing him coming back in. *"Then that couldn't be..."* She stopped again, as he walked right passed her, with not only a load of firewood in one arm, but a picture in his other hand.

Placing it up on the mantle, before starting on the fire, she saw it, as a barrage of pictures flashed passed her eyes, of a woman a lot like herself, smiling up at a man looking a lot like him. Once again she stopped to look up at him, only this time to see his expression sadden.

"What?" she asked, looking back at the picture he was taking back down to look at.

Slowly, everything about Catherine was beginning to come back to her.

"That..." she cried. *"That was... me...!"*

"Oh, Catherine... Lord, God, I will miss you and our little girl..."

"Catherine? Little... girl...? Oh, dear Lord..." she cried, pressing her hand to her own belly. *"Our ba...by..."* she began, but then realized she wasn't pregnant anymore. All at once, recalling the paper, and its date, as she covered her mouth, yet again and cried, *"I have been gone...! As in d...dead...? And my ba...by...! Oh, Go... I remember...! Oh, daddy... you said it was a girl. But what happened_____? Where is she_____?"* she wailed, as she flew out of the room, only to stop just in the foyer, where she came across a mirror hanging on the far wall. Gazing into it, all she could see was the reflection from what was behind her.

Not able to believe it, she forgot about the man in the other room, as he went to sit the picture back down, to pick up a piece of the newspaper.

Doing so, he caught sight of something white and willowy-looking in the foyer. Just then, his eyes locked with her tear-filled ones, and for an instant, it was as if his beloved Catherine had come back to him. However, if not for her long white colonial style dress, with its high-laced neckline, she would have been a spitting image of her. "Ca...Ca...Catherine...?" he cried, tear fully.

"What...?" she cried startledly, pulling back.

"P...please, don't go_____!" he called out, as she turned to flee the foyer, when heading for the grand staircase. "I won't hurt you! I promise! Just, please_____" he cried, "don't go_____!"

Feeling his heart about to break into millions of pieces, he took off in the same direction, hoping to find some sort of sign of her. When nearing the top of the staircase, he stopped to listen. It was then he heard the soft-like whimpers of a little girl at the far end of the hall. Going ever so quietly, so as not to frighten her, he reached the room inwhich the sound was coming from.

Pushing open the door a little, but just enough to see her lying across her bed, taken aback, he could not believe what he was seeing right before his very eyes. *'But it looks like Catherine, and yet...'* He stopped, as she rose to face him, while able to hear his thoughts. "Who are you?" he asked, attentively, while remaining just outside her room.

"Cy...Cynthia M...M...Morgan," she replied, catching her breath in short sobs. "And y...y...you...?"

Laughing, he replied, "Morgan Fairbanks. Catherine is... Was my wife, until she passed away while giving birth to our little girl! And from what I heard about you, your mother had too, as her mother, before her."

"Then I too have..."

"Died? I'm s...sorry." He stopped. "Man, this is crazy," he grinned, shaking his head.

"Why?" she asked, coming closer to her door.

"I was never one for believing in ghosts. Yet, with you, it's as if you are very real to me."

"Perhaps it is because I look like her."

"Are you, though? In some crazy mixed up way, is it possible that you had..."

"Reincarnated myself into your wife's life?"

"Yes."

"But why?"

"To be with your..." He stopped, wondering why he would say that.

"True love?" she finished.

"Yes. Wasn't his name, Michael?"

"You knew him?" she asked, not knowing what her father had done to him upon hearing of their relationship. To make matters worse, her pregnancy.

"Only from a brief story. From what I understand, your father was very protective of you, and didn't like any man taking you away from him."

"Yes, that is true," she replied, sadly. "Though, we were going to be married!"

"What happened?"

"I had received a wire, telling me that he must go."

"Go? Go where?"

"He never said."

"And I guess after that, you never saw him again?"

"No..." she began crying again.

"And the baby?"

"It was a..."

"Girl. Yes of course."

"After that, everything went black, until now."

"Then, had you lived my late wife's life, would you have remembered it?"

"No, I wouldn't think so, but then somehow I think I actually do remember bits and pieces of it."

"Oh?" He sounded hopeful.

"Yes, like how happy we were together. And in love...! We were so in love."

"Yes, more than life itself."

"I just wish I could remember more," she said, while willowing around in her room. "It seemed so brief."

"It felt so brief," he replied, when looking sadly at the floor, while running a hand over his hair. But then he heard someone calling out from the main floor, when turning back to see the frightened expression on her face. "What is it?" he asked, worriedly.

"Its..." She stopped, then upon hearing his name, with a sigh, she smiled, but why, she didn't know, as her life as Catherine was still very vague.

"Cynthia," he interrupted, worriedly, "will I see you again?"

"Uh huh," she smiled even more. "I will be here, *a l w a y s*..." her last word drifted out slowly, as she began to fade. "*J u s t w h i s p e r   m y   n a m e,   a n d   I   w i l l   c o m e...*"

Turning, he heard footsteps coming up the stairs, only now there were two sets of them.

"Morgan...?" Nate called out, while coming up with Jarred by his side.

"Here," he returned, coming away from Cynthia's room.

"Oh, good. We thought you had gotten spooked by one of the ghosts here," he teased.

"No, not spooked, exactly," he stopped to smile, as he looked back over his shoulder to see she had reappeared, only to smile warmly at him. With that, she curtsied and vanished once again, leaving him to his visitors.

Chapter Eleven

"Well, just the same, we came by to see if you were hungry," Jarred inquired, while the three of them headed back down to the parlor, where he went back over to get the fire started.

"Mary went and made us all some pot roast. So what do you say we set it up over here on the coffee table, until we can get this place cleaned up some?" Nate asked, while he and Jarred went about pulling the white sheets off the furniture, before laying out the food.

"Sounds fine by me! I guess I could stand to eat a bite, before going around to make up a list of what all needs to be fixed up around here."

"Sure. And if you're smart, you'll want to do that, before it gets too late," Jarred suggested, knowing something about the old plantation, that they didn't.

"Oh?" Morgan turned back to ask. Though, seeing something on this fairly large man's face, who was now sitting in one of the overstuffed chairs, he wondered what had him looking so nervous. "Jarred, is there something you care to share with us?"

"Me?" he groaned.

"Does it concern this old mansion?" Nate inquired, curiously.

"Well that all depends on what you have learned so far about this place."

"Not a heck of a lot," he returned. "I still have those papers to look over from Frank."

"Papers?" he asked.

"Yes. About Cat's past."

"How far back are we talking?" Nate asked, while going on to dish out the food.

Thinking what he and Cynthia were discussing, before they showed up, he didn't want to go into it just yet, but instead, just shrugged, "Oh, perhaps... back to her great-great-great grand-mother."

"Is that when it all started?" Jarred asked, puzzledly.

"I would assume so."

"No," Nate spoke up.

"What...?" Morgan asked, surprised. "What do you know of this?"

"Chief Ramsey, he knew of the..." He stopped suddenly.

"Curse?" Morgan began by laughing.

"Hey, how else can you explain it?"

"All right, just for the sake of argument, tell me."

"It was more like four great grandmothers ago, back in the 1840's, when Clarisa Haber-sham met the local psychic, a witch back in those days. They had become friends, and as friends, the girl told her of a great love that would come her way."

"A typical prediction. So what happened?" they asked.

"Oh, her great love did come all right. And get this, a Sea Captain, who the psychic herself had fallen in love with. But..."

"He would have nothing of her," Jarred guessed correctly.

"Yes. It seems that Clarisa's father took a keen liking to the man, and arranged for the marriage of their daughter to him. Thus making the witch thoroughly pissed."

"Oh, hell..." Morgan groaned. "I see where you are going with this."

"Yes. And one night, just before the marriage was to take place, the witch went off to her secret hiding place, and began some kind of spell of sorts, to curse all Habersham women, starting with Clarisa, once she became one."

"The curse that all firstborn children, which were to be girls, were to die giving birth to their own little girls?" Morgan asked. "It makes since. However, now that curse had ended with my Catherine, since our daughter had died, as well."

"It looks to be that way. Unless you were to marry another Habersham woman, and that's not likely, unless..."

"Unless what?" the two asked in unison.

"This Cynthia Morgan was to come back, claiming the life of a woman who was to have gotten into an accident, and did not want to live on any longer."

"Right. And why would she want to do that?" he asked, cynically.

"Because, according to Ramsey, you are the spitting image of her lost love."

"Who's that?" Jarred asked.

"Michael Fairington. Captain Michael Fairington. Honorable Sea Captain, like her father, and Veterinarian," Morgan explained. "But what I don't understand. If he were a Sea Captain, like Thaddeus Morgan, why did Thaddeus hate him so much to have him..." He stopped, not wanting her to overhear what he was about to say, in case she had never known what had happened to him, when the others picked up on his same concern.

"You have seen her, haven't you?" Nate asked, grinning.

Seeing his humor, he knew he couldn't keep the truth from him. "Yes, and God help me, she looks so much like Cat, in every way."

"Where is she now?" Jarred asked, getting to his feet to have a look around.

"Not here. Well at least, not at this time, anyhow."

Shaking his head sadly, Jarred dropped back down onto his chair.

"Thinking about your Cathy?" Morgan asked, seeing how he looked broken up at the thought of Cat's spirit being so close, yet it was Cynthia's now.

"I've really missed her over the years, and now..."

"Knowing that someone else looks so much like her...?"

"Yeah, it kinda bites."

"Maybe she will come around later," he grinned.

"Oh, yeah?"

"Yes, as I sort of picked up the expression on her face, when she saw you standing up there. At first, I didn't know why, but then, you and Cat were so close at one time. I think somewhere in her subconscious, she remembers that. Like she remembers our love."

"Then you're saying, she, in some way, is Cathy...?"

"Pretty much. Not to mention, something your sister had said earlier."

"Which was?"

"A psychic telling Cat, she was going to die, just like her mother, and her mother's mother."

"I remember that, and Lord, how that had upset her."

"I can see why, and especially once we had met, and fell so deeply in love."

"Yeah, well," Jarred added, seeming really uneasy just then, "there's one more thing that you must know."

"Yeah, well... out with it."

"Surely you have heard about the ghost of Captain Morgan?"

"No, what about him?"

"He's still here, and man, I wouldn't want to be in your shoes, when he sees you."

"Why is tha..." He stopped upon getting up to restoke the fire, when at that moment, seeing his own reflection in the mirror, above the fireplace, the answer came to him, "Oh, Christ, that's it, isn't it? I look like Fairington."

"An exact double of the man," he grinned, nervously. "And once Thaddeus sees you, he's going to..."

"Let me guess," he wailed abruptly, "raise the roof, sort of speak?"

"Oh... yeah."

"Great. And just when does he show himself?"

"Midnight," both Jarred and Nate announced, looking to each other just then.

"Oh, no, so that was it?" He thought once again about another expression he had seen on her face, when she first heard Jarred's voice call out.

"What?" Nate asked, concerned. "Had you already been visited by him?"

"No, but judging by the look on her face, when she first heard Jarred's voice, she looked as though she were about to run away. As if..."

"I was her father?"

"Yes, and no doubt, she's afraid of him."

"What are you planning to do?" Nate asked, knowing the look on his friends' face, all too well.

"You aren't..." Jarred spoke up, seeing it, too.

"Going to face him? Damn straight I am! But hopefully not alone."

"What...?" they both cried.

"Come on! You two aren't scared, are you?"

"Sc...sc...scared?" Jarred laughed. "Oh, *hell*... yes!"

"Come now, it's just a ghost!"

"A very bitter ghost," they both put in, looking to one another.

"Great, so much for having friends to stand by me, when I am about to get my butt kicked," he roared out heartily. "All right now, let's get done here so we can get started on this list of repairs, before witching hour starts in."

Having gotten their food eaten, the three headed out through the kitchen door.

"Where to first?" Nate asked.

"Well, with what all is going on with Jack Daniel's and the mare, I thought it would only be logical to start with the stables."

Taking Nate's Tahoe, they all got in and headed for the nearest stable, a rather long white building with three vented dorms on top for ventilation. The second building, like the first, looked as though it was going to take even more work, while looking even older than the first.

Once they finished the first of the three stables, seeing how the second was more out in the open, Nate asked, sensing if one of Copeland's men were to see the horses, he would know where they were being kept, "What about the third stable?"

"That'll have to come later," Morgan announced, "since we only have enough day light to get us through the second one."

Getting to the second stable, they all agreed that this would be the one to hide the two thoroughbreds in.

"And to throw off any suspicions," Morgan announced, "I will go out and pick up a few more so they will blend in."

"Good thinking," Jarred added. "And to help out, Scott and I will stay out in the bunkhouse so they're not left alone."

"Well, you won't be the only two staying. I have someone else coming in tomorrow to lend a hand. To add to it, I will be looking for a few more hands to help out around here. Now, as for this bunkhouse, where is it?"

"Over there," he pointed out to another weather-beaten building that no doubt needed working on.

"Great. Let's get this list made up, and quickly, so I can get started on it."

"What would you say, these two buildings? Meaning, this stable and the bunkhouse?" Nate asked, as he went about making a few notes of his own, as they walked on through the main entrance.

"Yes, and if the two of you can give me a hand, it will go a heck of a lot quicker. I know that Jason will lend his help when he arrives."

"What time will that be?" Nate asked.

"Between ten and noon."

"Great."

Having gotten that out of the way, they made their way through without another word, until reaching the bunkhouse.

"Man..." they all groaned at the dust and cobwebs that lurked all around them, but then stopped once they had gotten to the kitchen.

"Looks like someone's been staying out here," Morgan noted questioningly, as he turned to Jarred, "Any idea who?"

"Scott and I on several occasions, to get away from the Circle C."

"And that's how you knew about the place?"

"No," he mused. "My sister would come here with Cathy and her dog."

"Her dog?" he asked.

"Yeah, come to think of it, it looked a lot like your neighbor's dog. If I am not mistaken, I would have thought it was him. He had run off when the girls came across that third stable. Like he had seen a ghost."

"Come on with the ghost already," Morgan laughed. "Two is bad enough. And only one is welcome here as far as I'm concerned."

"Cynthia's?" they teased heartily.

"Who else?" he laughed along with them, while he went on around the room, stopping to check out the old wood stove. "I assume you've been keeping this up on repairs?"

"Sure, can't be havin none of them cold nights now, can we?" he returned with a larger than life grin.

Shaking his head, Morgan noted a few windows and a couple of floorboards that were in need of repair. "I guess then the plumbing all works?"

"Yep."

After seeing to the sleeping area, with its six beds, and six dressers, two of which needed some serious repairs, the three were off, and just in time, when walking out to see how the sun was about to set.

"Great, and none too soon," Nate announced, heading for the SUV.

"Yes," Morgan agreed, "and I have got to get back and light a few of those oil lamps to see by."

"So you're really going to stay the night then, aren't you?" Jarred asked, skeptically.

"Yes. Do I have any takers?"

"Nate?" Jarred turned.

"I don't know. Do we have any extra food in the place?"

"Sure, didn't you see the back end of the Tahoe?" Morgan teased. "I stopped off and grabbed a few things, before getting here."

"Great!" he laughed. "In that case how about I call Ramsey and see if he would like to join us? He's not afraid of ghosts!"

"Go right ahead," his friend agreed, as they headed back up to the house.

Once inside, after getting the lamps lit, Morgan took one up to his room, but then changing his mind, when he looked down the hall at Cynthia's. Going down to it, he stopped just outside her door to listen in. Not hearing anything, he was about to turn and walk away, but then, there it was, she was humming to a song quite similar to the one sang earlier.

Standing out in the hall quietly, he listened until it was over. At which, he turned back to knock softly at her door. "Cynthia...?" he called out quietly, so as not to be heard by the others, once Nate had gotten off his cell phone with Ramsey.

"Is he coming?" Jarred asked, hopefully.

"Yes, he will be here as soon as he makes a stopover at Madam Claries' place."

"To see what we're all in for here?"

Giving off a short laugh, he nodded his answer, "Uh, yes."

Meanwhile, upstairs, Morgan was showed into Cynthia's room, when closing the door behind him.

"You know, don't you?" she asked.

"About your father?"

"Yes. He will be very upset once he sees you here."

"So I have been told, but that isn't going to stop me. If he starts in on me, I will just have to fire back at him."

"B...but I don't want you to g...g...get..."

"What, Cynthia? You don't want me to get, what?"

Turning away to hide her tears, he began to wonder if she figured out what had happened to her lost love.

"You know, don't you?" he asked, reaching out to her, but then forgetting she was a spirit, just as his hand passed through her.

Chapter Twelve

"About Michael?" She turned back to see the grave look on his face. "I began to suspect it, when I was nearing my time to having our baby. He would have never stayed away from the birth of our child."

"Unless he had been detained, or..." He stopped, as she turned away to go over and throw herself onto her bed, crying.

Feeling the pain of her loss, as it hit him, he wanted to hold her, to offer her some sort of solace, but knew he couldn't. So, he simply sat softly next to her. "Cath..." he started, but then cleared his throat. "Cynthia, I'm sorry, I shouldn't have brought it up."

"No, you are right to do so. And too, I think I must have known something was wrong, when I first heard them arguing."

"What did you hear?"

"Daddy told him that he was a fool for not taking the money offered him, and leave when he had the chance."

"What money?"

Turning to look up at him, she wiped her tears away, and thought for a moment, as the whole scene played back in her mind. It was late one August evening, the two had just returned, slipping in through the kitchen door to head up to her room.

Seeing the cook, the old woman frowned at the two of them, and warned that they were playing with fire. Somehow her father had caught them once before, as their love was growing closer and closer, but that night he had overheard them talking about her impending pregnancy, and became enraged.

Having no more than closed the back door, Thaddeus Morgan spied them from around the corner of the kitchen doorway, as they were about to go up the back staircase. "*Michael...!*" he called out, walking in. Not saying another word, he glared hard at the veterinarian, before turning to head out of the kitchen, with Michael following behind.

"Fearing the worst, I waited until they left the room, before following them to daddy's den. Staying out of sight until after they had gotten the door closed, I went up to listen in."

"And that's when you heard the argument?"

"Yes, but then something happened. I had somehow lost my balance and started to fall into the door. I think they heard me and came to check it out."

"What did you do?"

"Well of course, I ran up to my room!"

"Did you see Michael after that?"

"No. I heard the slamming of the front door, before going to bed."

Shaking his head, he pondered the thought of what he had learned earlier. '*Had he went to one of his stable hands and ordered his death?*' he thought, unaware she could pick up on them.

"No...!" she cried, shaking her head. "No...!"

Just then, they heard some footsteps coming up the stairs, as she started to look frighten

ed again.

"Take it easy," he offered, softly. "It's probably one of my friends, coming up to check on me."

He was right, but it wasn't only his two friends, but Ramsey and one other, as well.

Going to the door, he went out to see what was going on. At that time his eyes fell upon the same dog that was in the clinic earlier. "What?" he asked, just as the dog stopped at his feet, but not to look up at him, but the woman standing in behind him.

"Spooks...!" she cried out, so that not only he and Morgan would hear her, but see her as well.

Not thinking, he looked to her questioningly, "You know him?"

"M...M...Morgan...?" Jarred spoke up, half puzzledly, at what he had just done.

"Oh, crap!" Morgan turned back to see all faces looking at him.

"Who were you just talking to?" Jarred asked, curiously.

"Me...?" he pointed, sheepishly.

Then Cynthia looked up and saw Jarred for herself, as bits and pieces of Catherine's memories began to play back in her mind. "J...Jarhead...?" she cried, tearfully.

Again, Morgan was the only one to hear her, when he looked back to see her starring off at Jarred. "Oh, no."

"What?" Nate asked this time.

"She remembers him from your late wife's memory of her childhood," Ramsey explained, sensing her presence.

"You can see her, as well?" Morgan asked.

"No. But I can feel her nearby."

"Cathy...? I m...mean, Cynthia?" Jarred asked, while fighting back his own tears at how much he had missed his little brat.

"Well?" Morgan turned back, as she was coming into full solidity.

"I can't stay this way for long, or I will soon run out of energy and have to go."

"Oh, God," both Jarred and Nate fell back a step, as she smiled warmly at the two.

"Hello, Jarhead," she teased, laughingly.

"Same to you, brat," he returned, wishing how he could go to her and hold her.

Once again, she picked up on his thoughts, as well, and went up to softly place her left hand alongside his tear-dampened face.

Doing so, he felt the tingling sensation of her touch, and smiled, "I can feel that!"

"What...?" Morgan asked, surprised. "But how...?"

"It's her electrical field that she puts off," Ramsey offered. "All spirits have them, and especially if the other person is the slightest bit wet. At which they will really feel it."

"But it doesn't hurt," Jarred replied.

"No. And with her, it won't," he went on. "She is a loving spirit, not like her father, Thaddeus."

Just at the mention of her father, she pulled away fearfully.

"No, Cynthia," Morgan interceded. "He isn't here yet, and when he does get here, you won't be alone to face him."

"But..."

"But, nothing," he reassured her, softly. "We will all be here for you. You can count on that."

Hearing his words of kindness, a smile returned to her pretty face, as they went on talk
ing. But then, the subject about the dog came up.

"I don't quite understand. How did you know the dog, and he know you?"

"He's her protector," Ramsey again offered.

"Sent to me by my mother, from what I was told by some man in the city. An old Indian, I believe," she finished.

"Ramsey?" They all turned to look to him.

"My great grandfather," he explained, "he knew of the curse, and was given the dog to watch over her."

"But this dog is alive! Now, how can he be, having belonged to my late wife, and been hers, as well?"

"Oh, but he isn't. Just look at him. Look into his eyes," he said, pointing to the dog.

Doing that, Morgan knelt down, shaking his head at what he had seen. "It is as if..." he began numbly.

"Yes, as if you are looking right into heaven. Though, you can't see it, you can only feel it deep within yourself."

"And now?"

"He is back to protect her from her father, when he returns each night at midnight."

"What time is it now?" Nate was asking.

"Nine-twenty. You still have time before he returns. But," Ramsey stopped to study Morgan warningly, "you of all the others are in more danger than she is."

"Because of my likeness to Michael?"

"Yes."

"M...Morgan..." she began to cry.

"No, he won't hurt me. Nor will he scare me away. I mean it, Cynthia, I am not going anywhere."

"And we will be here, as well," Jarred spoke up, protectively.

"That won't be on all cases," Ramsey warned.

"What are you saying now?" Morgan asked, heatedly.

"There will come a time that you..." He stopped, as he recalled something the local psychic told him, before he arrived.

"That I, what?"

"It isn't you," he said, looking right into his eyes.

"What are you babbling about, it isn't me?"

"No. It is you, but it isn't," he replied, shaking his head. "Something is going to happen to you soon. Not tonight, but very soon indeed."

"Great. More hocus-pocus."

"No hocus or pocus, but it's time."

"Ramsey, what are you saying?" Nate asked, worriedly.

"Along time ago, your friend here had felt as though he were missing a piece of his life. He was correct on that assumption. A piece of his life, or I should say his soul, has been missing, and not yet been found."

"My soul...?" he scorned, disbelievingly. But he knew deep down what this old Indian was saying. At one time, he had felt lost, as if there were an empty void in his heart. Then Catherine came into his life, and since then, he had felt whole, or at least he did for the time being.

"You know, don't you?" Ramsey asked, smiling.

"Y...yes, I remember now." He looked away momentarily.

"Morgan, are you all right?" Nate asked, as he went up to take him by the arm.

"Yes," he answered blankly. "I had just forgotten, is all."

"Then, it's true...?"

"Back in college, just before Cat came along," he returned, looking to Ramsey. "What's going to happen to me now?"

"I can't say for sure, but as it does, you will certainly feel a jolt to your senses, and might even feel sickened by it. Whatever you do, or any of you who sees this happening to him, just let it take its course."

At that time, Cynthia began to waver, as her time with them was coming to a brief end.

Seeing this, Morgan was beginning to understand what was happening to her, as she was fading in and out on them. "You have to go, don't you?"

"Yes, but I will be back. I promise."

"Miss Cynthia," Ramsey called out, before she could fade away completely, "I was told that when your father does come, not to be afraid, but until you can face him, simply go into hiding. Your protector will do the rest. As he will also do for you, Mr. Fairbanks," he turned.

"Me?"

"Oh, yes, since you look a great deal like the man, Thaddeus hates most, all because of his daughter."

"M...Morgan..." she was getting more and more transparent now, *"p...please... be careful of him..."* she implored him, as she vanished completely to store up her energy so she could return to be near him.

That night, everyone found where they were going to sleep, as most of them chose to stay down in the parlor, near the fireplace to stay warm. Morgan, on the other hand, went to his own

room, located in the middle of the mansion, near hers.

Soon after everyone slipped off to sleep, just as Ramsey said, the spirit of Thaddeus Morgan appeared in his navy blue wool overcoat, hovering overhead. Puzzled at what he saw sprawled out over the parlor, the tall, burly, old sea Captain moved on to check out the rest of his home.

Meanwhile, up in Morgan's room, Spooks stayed close to watch over his new master, when the air suddenly became cold as ice, as Thaddeus appeared in the doorway.

Seeing the man lying waist deep beneath the quilt, with a light sheen of perspiration across his back, the old man had no idea it was from Morgan having been dreaming of his late wife during that time. "W h a t_____ i s_____ t h i s_____?" his voice thundered, while rumbling the whole mansion, when waking the others, as Morgan slept on, while lying on his stomach, with both arms tucked up under his pillow.

Hearing this, Spooks began growling toward their predator away.

"*Blast it dog, you will not be rid of me so easily,*" he glared.

Standing his territory, the dog continued, with his back hairs rising up like quills on a porcupine, while moving closer to the aberration.

Seeing this, Thaddeus knew he could not scare him off, when he left, heading for his daughter's room, where she came back just in time to sense his presence.

"Oh, no...!" she cried quietly, when at that precise moment, her room became as cold as the other one.

Meanwhile, downstairs, with all his Indian upbringing, Ramsey got up from his bedroll, feeling Thaddeus's presence and went to the grand staircase to begin chanting to ward off the evil spirit.

Seeing this, the others began to utter their own prayer, while upstairs Spooks appeared in her room to ward off Thaddeus's spirit, once again.

"This time, dog, you won, but not for long. I will be back. You_____ hear_____ me_____? I will be back_____!" With that, he was gone.

Looking around for his mistress, Spooks let out a soft, but friendly bark, to tell her she was safe.

Hearing him, she appeared, and went over to hug him dearly. "Oh... thank you, boy. You have done your job well," she cooed, before releasing him to return to the other room, where she too went to be closer to Morgan.

There, she was reminded of her love, when seeing just how masculine Morgan's back looked. Having not seen a man's bare back in so long, even in her memory as Catherine, that part of her life seemed blocked out. Nevertheless, going over to be near him, she was unaware that beneath the quilt, he was wearing nothing, when he went to turn over to get more comfortable.

Meanwhile, watching him breath, she smiled softly, as she went on to lie in next to him, thinking about Michael, while the others returned to their own bedrolls at Ramsey's insistence.

Chapter Thirteen

The next morning, before the others got up, all but Ramsey, who was in the kitchen preparing coffee and breakfast, Morgan woke to the sound of a woman's soft breathing. Looking over to his left, for a moment, it was as if he were looking upon the beautiful face of his beloved wife. At that, even then he had thought that her death was all just a nightmare. But then, as she went to raise her arms up over her head to stretch, the vision changed, as she looked up into his troubled expression.

"Mmmm... Morgan, what is it?" she asked, raising up to face him.

"Nothing," he replied, as his smile returned to his handsome face, while bringing one onto hers. "I was just about to grab a shower," he explained, while going on to getting up.

Suddenly, she let out a cry, covering her eyes, at what she saw, when he stood up.

"What is it?" he quickly asked, looking back.

"Y...y...you...!" she pointed with one hand, while keeping the other over her eyes.

Looking down at his naked body, even his libido stood aroused at her very own beauty. Slightly embarrassed, he offered an apology, "I'm sorry, I assumed you and Michael had seen each other at one point or another."

"No, he had always kept the lights down low, knowing how shy I was."

"Oh?" Grabbing up his jeans, he smiled, while quickly pulling them on. "There you go, all covered now."

Taking her hands down slowly, she looked back to see him standing there, grinning down at her. "You must think I am silly," she giggled.

"No. You can't help but be shy. I think that is kinda cute."

"Really?"

"Yes. My wife was the same way." After saying what he did, he shook his head, grinningly. "But then you would know that, wouldn't you?"

Smiling even brighter, she nodded her head. "Uh huh."

"I miss her, you know? And seeing you, I sometimes want to call you by her name."

"As I want to call you, Michael."

"Would it matter if I were to ever..." He stopped to turn away.

"Say it," she prompted, knowing full well what was in his heart, when seeing the look in his eyes.

"I can't. It wouldn't be fair to you."

"Maybe not, but if it helps."

Feeling her gentle spirit reaching out to him, he offered her a warm loving smile, before turning to head for the bathroom, where turning on the water, using more hot than cold, he stood under its rigorous flow to try and focus on what all he needed to do that day.

Meanwhile, downstairs, the others were slow to get up, when Jarred offered to go over and get another fire going to warm it up a little. "Smells like bacon cooking," he announced, feeling his stomach rumble.

"And coffee, too," Nate agreed.

"Do you think Morgan made it through the night all right?"

"I hope so. That, and Ramsey seems to think so."

"Because of what the psychic had to say?"

"Sure. And I have a feeling that he has some sort of gift, as well. He told me a while back his father and his grandfather were both shaman?"

"That would explain his gift with animals," Nate agreed.

"Yep," he acknowledged, while getting things straightened up around the quaint decent sized parlor, when hearing Morgan come down the main staircase.

"Good morning!" he called out, joining them. "And how was our evening last night?"

"You don't know!" Nate returned, looking to Jarred, surprisingly.

"Know what?" he asked, looking at the two of them, before going into the other room.

"Thaddeus," Jarred began. "He was here, just as predicted."

"Hell, I must have slept right through it."

"Must have," the two agreed, while walking on into the kitchen with him.

Looking up, Ramsey saw Morgan's bright smiling face. "You look well this morning. Get enough rest?"

"Yes. Though I heard I slept right through our visitor last night. How did it go for the rest of you?" he asked, while going over to pour himself some coffee.

Joining him, Nate shook his head, "I can't believe you didn't wake up to the sound of the house rumbling. Thaddeus was really angry at our being here."

"Come on, Nate," Jarred teased. "We both know it was Morgan he was mad at."

"Oh," Ramsey spoke up, while carrying over a couple of plates of food, "but it wasn't
only that."

"What?" they asked, puzzledly.

Turning, they all saw Spooks enter the kitchen, wagging his tail, when going over to sit next to Morgan.

"Your servant awaits you," Ramsey grinned, while going over to fetch him some bacon off the platter.

"My servant?" Morgan asked, while turning to grin down at the dog lovingly.

"Oh, but of course, and your protector, as well. Now there is the real reason behind Thaddeus's anger last night. He knows that he can't hurt you, or even get close to his daughter with Spooks here to watch over you."

"Great. You hear that Spooks? Stay close by us at all times, all right?"

"Rrrr...uff!" he responded happily, before chowing down on his own breakfast.

"Ramsey," Jarred turned, "if he is a spirit dog, how can he eat like a normal one?"

"He's special in a unique sort of way. Here on earth he is real. Though in dangerous situations, he takes on a spirit form so as not to be hurt."

"Well, either way, I'm glad he is here," Morgan replied, as he hurried down his food to get a start on his morning.

Once done, he got to his feet to go in and get a pad of paper and pen from the wood paneled den. Stopping at the doorway on his way out, it made him think back on something she had said about the argument between her father and Michael. '*All right, Thaddeus, if you had him killed, where did you have it done, and where is he now?*' he wondered, before heading for the kitchen to go out the back door.

"Heading out already?" his friends called out from the large table in the center of the room.

"Yeah. Just take your time, though. Oh, and Nate?" he called from the back door.

"Yeah?"

"Jason will be here shortly. How about bringing him out with you guys, when he does?"

"Sure! Stable three?" he asked.

"Yes, since it will probably need the most work. Anyway I am going on out to get started on making out a list."

"See ya then," his friend returned, downing his coffee, before getting up to get another.

Walking on out, but not alone, Spooks went along with him. "Yeah, I kinda thought so, boy. So what do you think, too beautiful of a day to drive over?" he laughed, while seeing the dog gaze up at him so trustingly. "Yeah, me too," he concluded, while choosing to walk instead.

Arriving at the second stable, Morgan knew he had seen a lane, which led back to the third stable just the other day. Finding it overgrown with weeds, with a little work on his part, he went back to get a cycle he saw in the first stable, and had gotten at least halfway down the path, when he stopped to take a rest.

"Well, Spooks, I can see right now how this is going to have to be cut, before we can even get started on the work at hand," he said, while writing it down on his list of things to do. However, just ahead was his real work, as the two went on to walk a little closer. As he did, they saw it from a short distance away, three dormers protruding through a vast amount of heavy overgrowth of vines. "The third stable," he groaned, seeing its run down condition. "Great, just wait until the others get here," he continued, while walking on up to it.

Getting even closer, he looked to see where the entrance was, in comparison to the other two stables. Seeing how this one was quite similar, it was made painfully clear that it had been boarded up for some time. As the old weather-beatened doors themselves had, weather-beatened, two by fours nailed over them, not to mention, an overgrowth of vine, as well.

"Damn," he grumbled, knowing he hadn't brought anything with him to pry them open.

Looking back at the house, he didn't much relish the idea of walking all the way back to get some tools. Lucky for him, just at the base of the doors, was what appeared to be an old rusted pry bar, buried slightly beneath some settled mud and dirt.

"This ought to do it. What do you think, boy?" he grinned.

Once again, he got his reply, as his companion let out a soft response, before the two started to dig it out.

After doing so, once a lot of the vines had been pulled away, he applied the bar to each one of the boards, removing them, as he went along. Then came the old rusty pad lock. Applying the bar directly to the center of the catch, he gave it a try, but it didn't budge. Trying it repeatedly, the lock finally broke free. However, the doors remained unmoved.

"Okay..." he grumbled once again, while looking them over with one hand holding the pry bar propped on his hip the back of the other, wiping the sweat away from his brow. "Must be something keeping them from coming open. But what?" he wondered clearly, while not quite ready to call it quits, just yet.

At that time, placing a small amount of spit on each hand, before rubbing them together, he located the right place to pull. As he did, without warning, one of the doors broke free due to more overgrowth than he had noticed. As it did, a blast of air, mixed with dirt and a dry stale smell, which he wasn't familiar with, hit him so hard it had knocked him off his feet.

Falling to the ground, he became so dazed that while trying to clear his sight, pictures of someone else's past hit him like a ton of bricks. "W...w...what is happening to me?" he groaned miserably, as the scenes went on before him, with workmen, dressed in old clothes, walking all around him, in what looked to be an old horse's stable. Then everything went black around him, when he, himself, fell hard to the ground, rendering himself unconscious. Until when? He never knew, as Spooks could only sit, while watching over him.

"Orr... Orr... Orr..." the dog mourned, while going up to nuzzle his cold nose to Morgan's face.

Meanwhile, up at the house, a knock sounded at the front door. Going to see who it was, Nate burst out laughing at the sight of their old friend, Jason, standing there, holding a large suitcase in each hand. "Jason... is that really you...?"

Looking somewhat surprised at seeing him there, and so early in the morning, the policeman from Cool Water, West Virginia broke out, as well, "Well, if it isn't Nathaniel Winslow. I thought I would find Morgan here, not you...!"

"Yeah, well he's out checking on the last stable, while we were just waiting on you, before heading out to give him a hand."

"We?" he asked, puzzledly. "Not Steve and his family, I gather, because they are still back home, trying to get everything wrapped up, before coming down."

"No," he explained, taking a suitcase, before closing the door behind them. "We, as in Chief Ramsey and Jarred here," he pointed, as the others walked out of the kitchen to join him. "Jason, meet Chief Ramsey, the one for which I had taken over for at the animal clinic. And Jarred Ashford, Cat's... Well, you might call him, her adopted big brother. His sister was her best friend back in high school."

"Chief," Jason offered his hand to shake, as he then turned questioningly to the tall, husky man next to him. "Jarred," he went on to shake his hand, as well, but reserved judgment on this particular one, as Morgan had told him that he worked for Copeland.

"I see you don't quite trust me," Jarred offered, seeing how Jason's eyes narrowed at the sight of him.

"Do I dare?" he asked.

"When you get to know me, yes."

"Jason," Nate cut in, "we will fill you in on the way out to the third stable. For now, let's just get you settled in."

"We should wait on that," Ramsey spoke up suddenly.

"Oh?" The others who knew him, picked up right away on his concern, as they ditched Jason's things off to one side of the foyer to head out through the kitchen.

115

Seeing how his Tahoe was still parked in the same place, they all jumped in and headed out to the last stable.

"What's the hurry?" Jason asked, as Nate tried to take each rut along the lane carefully.

"When Chief Ramsey looks worried," Jarred spoke up, sitting next to him, "that usually means trouble."

Right away, suspecting trouble may be coming their way, Jason opened his vest enough to place a hand over his concealed service revolver. Though not wanting Jarred see he carried one, he kept it hidden away.

"Guys..." Nate called out just as they appeared at the top of an incline, when the third stable came into view. "Is that..."

"Morgan...?" Jason cried out, before anyone else could. While just out front of the third stable was Morgan's body, sprawled out on the ground, where it remained, after he collapsed. Next to him, was Spooks, still keeping close tabs on him.

Seeing this, Nate increased his speed to get to him. Once there, he was first to get out, and rush over to see what had happened. "Morgan_____! Morgan_____!" he cried out at the top of his lungs. Upon reaching him, he immediately checked for a pulse.

"Nate, what could have done this to him?" Jason asked first, when the others had caught up.

"I don't have a clue. All I can say is that he is still with us, thank God. But his pulse is really out there."

"Is that bad?" Jason asked.

"Well, if we don't get him to come around!" He thought for a moment. "I can't say for sure. Nevertheless, no, I don't think so. It looks like he is trying to come around now."

"Who could have done this to him?" Jason asked, while looking over their surroundings, along with Jarred, who had suspected one of Copeland's other men having done this themselves. "Any signs of foul play?" he went on.

"I can't tell," Nate offered, with a great deal of concern in his voice.

Meanwhile, while the others tended to their friend, Ramsey picked up on something coming from the old building. Getting to his feet, he went over to have a look. But then stopping upon reaching the doors, he turned back to see Morgan's body twitching from side to side, and knew what had taken place. "No_____" he called back, when returning to kneel before him.

"What?" they asked.

"You mustn't try to move him."

"Why?" Nate went on to ask.

"Remember Nathaniel, what I told you the other night."

Looking back on at his friend, Nate repeated Ramsey's warning, "If any of us see him like this, do not try and move him."

"I don't understand," Jason spoke up. "What are you talking about? See him like this. What is going on? And what the hell is wrong with me friend?"

"It's a long story," Nate returned, while watching Morgan closely.

Doing the same, they all sat quietly, as Morgan continued to twitch back and forth, as more visions came flashing before him. One particular one was of his love cradled in his arms. But was it Catherine? Or was it Cynthia? The clothing was all somehow different, as well as the hairstyle. And then, that God awful argument with an overbearing man in his late fifties, which led to the workmen, and then a sudden bone crushing blow reaching out of nowhere, which ended up in total darkness.

"Morgan...?" Nate called out, seeing his eyes begin to flutter open. "Morgan... can you hear me? It's Nate. Jason is here with me, along with Ramsey and Jarred."

"Mmmm..." he moaned, while raising a hand weakly to his head.

"Take it easy. You've been unconscious for some time now," Jason said, stopping him.

"Mmmm..." he moaned again. "W...where am... I?"

"The stables," Nate explained, while helping him up into a seated position. As he did, Morgan wavered a bit, before they went to lay him back down.

"It's still too soon," Ramsey offered, while getting a closer look at him. "We should let him lie still a bit longer, before trying to move him, just yet."

Just as he was about to come closer, Morgan looked up at him and flinched back with wide eyes.

Seeing this, there was no doubt something indeed had happened, as Ramsey kept it to himself for the time being.

"Ramsey... what is it?" Nate asked, sensing something from him, just then.

"Wait," he motioned with a hand held to them, as he continued to study the man's baffled expression, while he remained lying on the ground.

Meanwhile, looking even more puzzled, he continued to look up, though not only at Ramsey, but the others, until he was finally able to sit up again.

Staying quiet, Spooks watched and waited for the right time to approach his master.

"Morgan..." Nate spoke up again, "are you all right?"

"M...M...Morgan...?" he groaned, just above a whisper. "Mmmm..." he moaned, rubbing at his head again.

"Take it easy, we'll have you back up at the house in no time," Jarred offered, as he and the others got up to lend him a hand.

Still shaken over what had happened, it took both Nate and Jarred to get him up to the Tahoe, once Jason brought it closer.

Once they got him back to the house, they immediately took him up to his room and laid him down.

"He should rest awhile, before looking him over again," Nate explained, while looking at his friend worriedly. "Whatever happened out there, it had to have knocked him out pretty hard."

"Yes, but what?" Jason and Jarred both asked, while standing at the end of the bed, not seeing Cynthia, as she came in upon hearing their voices.

Seeing Morgan lying so weakly in his bed, she wanted to cry out, but waited until the others had left.

Her wait wasn't long. With the insistence of Ramsey, at seeing her looking so frantic, he ushered the others out, while closing the door behind him.

Chapter Fourteen

Going to him, Cynthia looked deep within his hazy eyes, as they turned to see her tears streaming down her cheeks.

"M...M...Muffet...?" he called out to her in a soft-like whisper, though not loud enough to be heard, as his hand found its way to her tear-dampened cheek.

Feeling it, she jumped up with a start at how it had felt to her. "W...w...what just happened?" she cried, touching her hand to the same spot. "I shouldn't have felt that!"

"Why on earth not?" he asked.

"M...M...Morgan... you're not..."

"M...Morgan?" he questioned again. "Who is this Morgan? And why on earth is everyone calling me that?"

Suddenly, hearing a slight change in his voice, her tears came even more, as he went to take her hand. "No..." she cried out frightenedly, when his hand slipped right through hers.

As it did, he fell back onto his pillow for a moment in silence, while his eyes went blank. Soon though they started to flutter. "Cyn...thia?" he groaned aimlessly when hearing her cry, which had snapped him out of what had taken over him previously. "H...how did I get up here?"

"Your friends brought you up. Don't you remember?"

"No...! All I re...remember is prying that God awful door open."

"Door?"

"Down at the last stable. It had been boarded up."

"The one with..." She stopped to sit back down on the edge of the bed, at the recollection of the third stable from when she was Catherine.

"The vines growing all over it? Yes," he offered, when attempting to sit up.

"Y...yes...?"

"Well, whatever the reason for it being boarded up, the air itself had knocked me off my feet pretty hard. Afterwards, all I remember was a lot of stuff from the past. God help me, it was as if it were someone else's past, and not mine!"

"Someone else's?" she asked, when then it hit her, as he had called her by her nickname earlier. One in which only Michael had called her. Looking down at his hand, it was lying within her own, as if at one time holding it. Even then, recollecting when he had actually touched her cheek, she began to wonder frightfully. *'What is happening here?'*

"Cynthia... what is it?" he asked, as she went to get up and walk over to the door.

"Don't you know?" She stopped to look back at him.

"Know? Know, what? What are you talking about?"

"When they brought you in. I saw how pale you looked. Then after they left, I went to you, crying. I was so afraid that something had happened to you. Then you looked at me, and... and... and... you called me, M...Muffet! Only one man has ever called me that."

"M...Michael?" he said hesitantly.

"Yes. M...Michael."

"Oh, my God..." he groaned, shaking his head. "The stables. That's it!" he continued to groan, while getting to his feet.

"Where are you going?" she cried, following after him, as he stumbled out the door.

"Back to the last stable. Michael..."

"What about him?" she asked, cutting him off.

"He must have been there. Because, when I had finally gotten the doors open, a blast of stale air hit me so hard that it knocked me off my feet. It was then that all those visions started up in my head. I thought it was my late wife that I was cradling in my arms, but it was you! You and Michael. Not me and Catherine."

"But the letter?" she cried.

"It had to have been a fake. Or worse yet, he was forced to have written it."

"And then..."

"Your father had him..."

"No_____!" Her voice rang out over the entire house, while bringing everyone downstairs to their feet in a hurry.

"God, girl, I'm sorry. I don't know what else I can say!"

"Not Michael_____!" she wailed heavily, and faded away, when his friends came running up the stairs to see him turning to come down them.

"Morgan_____?" they each called out, as he pushed passed them.

"The stables_____!" he yelled back over his shoulders. Though at the bottom of the stairs he turned back to Jason, "I'm going to especially need you."

"Why? What's going on?" he asked, while heading down after him, as Morgan turned to head for the back door.

"I'll fill you in on the way. Ramsey..." He stopped in the kitchen, "if you know of anyone who can keep their mouths shut in the Coroner's Office, we are going to need them. And Nate?"

"Call Brice, I presume?"

Smiling, he shook his head. "It's Michael! I think I know just where he is!"

"Oh, but he is a lot closer then you think," Ramsey muttered, barely beneath his breath, when he went to place the call.

Going on out with Jason and Jarred at his side, Morgan looked around for the Tahoe. "Where is it?"

"Where's what?" Jarred asked.

"The Tahoe?"

"Up front!" Jason offered.

"Come on," Jarred insisted, as he ran for the black vehicle he had kept hidden away, "we can use the Bronco!"

Getting in, they headed for the last stable, while Morgan searched in the glove box for a flashlight. Taking it out, he turned to his friends, "When we get there, I'm going to need the two of you to start pulling away at the vines along the windows. We need all the light we can get."

"And you?" Jason asked.

"I'm going in to have a look around."

Having been told about the Cynthia Morgan story, Jason didn't argue, just nodded his head, as they reached their destination.

Getting out, Jarred went around back to pull out some tools he had covered up in the back end of his vehicle. "Here," he called out, holding up a couple of hatchets, "these might come in handy."

"Great!" Jason returned, laughing, when taking one. "You come prepared, don't you?"

"Well, you never know out here. Though I hear they are useless against big bad ghost who like to come calling at midnight," he grinned, closing the back end.

"Funny. Real funny," Jason laughed, while the two went on around to the north side of the building to get started, while Morgan went to the front door.

Finding it still open from earlier, Morgan felt a deep sense of sadness hit him, before going in. "Lord, whatever we find, help us to piece together what had happened here all those years ago," he prayed, just as he reached out to run a hand over one of the first stall doors he came to. After taking a few more steps in, he stumbled onto something near the third stall door, just as one of the side windows came open to shine some light in on the object. "J...J...Jason_____!" he called out, seeing what it was. "J...Jason_____! I need you in here_____! Now_____!"

Running in with Jarred at his side, the two stopped to see a set of bones at his feet.

"Morgan..." Jason swallowed hard, as he stopped to stare down at the skeleton laying beside a smaller set of bones.

"Looks like a dog," Jarred suggested, not seeing the other set of bones lying not far from it, when he went down on bended knees to check it out.

Finally turning on the flashlight since getting there, Morgan stood looking at the cause of the stale air, as he too had to swallow hard. "Oh, dear God in Heaven," he groaned, just as he had to turn away, when another flash of the past hit him unexpectedly. With it, he found himself having to slump down to the ground, while bringing up his knees to his chest, and his head against the wall.

"Morgan..." Jason looked up to check on is friend, once he was through looking over the remains of the dog. "Hey, you all right there, buddy?"

Pointing it out to him, both Jason and Jarred turned slowly to see what he was pointing at.

"Oh, my God!" the two pulled back at seeing the bony hand of a man's skeletal remains stretched out before them, and on it was a ring baring the navy insignia.

Following the hand up to what was left of the man's rotted coat, Jason shook his head bewilderedly. "Michael Fairington, I presume."

Taking a closer look at the ring, he stopped to look over at Morgan.

"What?" Morgan asked, seeing where his attention had fallen.

"Your ring!" he began, then looking back down at the other, he shook his head again. "It's the same! And on the same hand, as well!"

Rolling the poor fellow over ever so carefully, Morgan leaned forward as something shinny fell out of its pocket. "Wait. What was that?" he called out.

"What?" the two asked, looking puzzled.

Getting up to move around Michael's remains, Morgan sifted through the dirt, until he found what had slipped out.

"What is it?" Jarred asked, while looking intently over his shoulders.

"It's a ring!" he returned, holding it up in the light. "To be precise, it looks to have been an engagement ring."

"Cynthia's?" Nate asked, appearing in the doorway, when he and Ramsey arrived to see what they had found.

"Yes. And I know just what needs to be done with it," he turned to his friends.

"Don't say it," Jason grinned, knowingly. "Give it to the woman's ghost, I bet?"

"Yes. And if I know her, she will want to see him before he is taken away to be placed next to her, in the family plot."

"Then the hauntings will come to a happy end?" Nate concluded.

"No, not just yet," Ramsey added. "There is still the matter of Thaddeus's ghost. And now that Morgan has set Michael's spirit free of its prison..."

"He has a score to settle with him?" Morgan announced. As he did, something registered in his eyes, as only Ramsey could see.

"Yes. And as you recall my telling you the other night..." Ramsey reminded.

"Something was going to happen to change my life," Morgan concluded.

"And it has, hasn't it?" he asked, sensing Michael's presents in Morgan when he spoke.

"Yes, I...I think so."

"What...?" Nate and Jason wanted to know.

"The visions of another man's life. One who looks a great deal like me. And up in my room, after you all left, she came to me with tears in her eyes."

"Cynthia?" all but Ramsey asked.

"Yes. Even stranger than that, I touched her cheek. Or at least he did. And she felt it too!"

"What else?" Nate asked, seeing the glow on Morgan's face.

"He had even called her by the nickname that he had given her all those years ago. Which reminds me, I did the same with Catherine, just before getting her to the hospital. Heck I wondered, then, why! And now I'm beginning to see!"

"What are you feeling now?" Ramsey asked.

"Confusion, as to who I am. I can remember my own life, and now I'm having to remember his, as well! It's as if a big part of me that I had been missing out on has come home to rest!"

"Are you in any kind of pain?" Nate asked, taking on a more medical means of approach, while going up to take Morgan's pulse.

"No. It's wild. I can't explain it."

"Then let it happen," Ramsey offered. "Yours and Michael's spirit will soon be as one.

As he has to settle the score with her father, and too, you have to save two innocent horses."

"But what do I know about horses? Other than riding them."

"Michael's spirit will help you with that. Soon it will be as if you were born to be a..."

"No. Don't say it," he roared out with laughter.

"Yes, Morgan," Nate teased. "The V word. You're going to become a..."

"Veterinarian?" Jarred teased.

By then they all laughed just as a vehicle approached the stable.

Hearing it, everyone had gotten seriously quiet, as Jason went for his service revolver.

Meanwhile, going over to peer out the side window, with Jarred standing right behind them, to their relief, it was Brice, and a man only Ramsey knew, with him.

Going out to greet them, Ramsey went up to shake the old man's hand. "Stadler, it's good to see you, my old friend."

"And you, as well. Now, what do we have here?" he asked, walking in to have a look.

"It's our young vet, Michael Fairington, and what appears to be a dog lying next to him," Ramsey explained.

"Ahhh, the Morgan's old dog," he nodded.

"Wait a minute," Morgan and Jarred both replied.

"Are you saying this is Spooks?" Jarred then asked, shockingly.

"Yes," the Coroner replied, knowing the story. "The young lady's father had the dog shot after she had passed away, and placed with the vet. You might just say; to keep the ole' lad company."

"And the one we have been seeing lately?" they asked.

"Like I said," Ramsey grinned. "Her protector, and now yours, as well," he smiled quietly at Morgan, while they headed out of the stable to let Brice and the Coroner do their job, when the coroner went back to get a body bag out of the back of his car.

Moments later, when the two men were coming out with Michael's remains, Morgan turned to Mr. Brice, and asked, "This will be kept quiet, won't it?"

"Yes, extremely quiet," he bowed his head. "And as to his burial?"

"I want him next to Cynthia Morgan's, where he belongs."

"But of course," the man smiled warmly, as the two went on to place the remains in the back of Brice's hearse, before taking their leave.

"Morgan," Nate spoke up, "weren't you wanting to, you know," he pointed up at the house.

"Damn, you're right." Stopping the two men, he fought to think of how to ask what was sure to sound strange. Then he smiled and proceeded to explain his need to have a proper burial. "Gentlemen, I know how this must sound, but I would like to hold an impromptu funeral for him up at the house, if you don't mind, before you take him away."

"Sir?" the Coroner looked surprised.

"You heard me. He deserves having a showing of sorts after what had happened to him. Let's just call it, closure, shall we?"

Doing as they were asked, everyone headed up to the house, as Morgan went on ahead of them to prepare Cynthia for what was to take place.

Chapter Fifteen

Not feeling all that comfortable with the idea of having a showing for a man that had been dead for over one hundred years, Morgan gave the suggestion of bringing in a temporary casket, done up so not to look too morbid. Soon, with the help of Jarred's sister, they were able to draw up a composite of Michael, using Morgan as a model, to show how he would have looked back then.

By eight-thirty, everyone, meaning those who had seen Cynthia, and now Brenda and her mother, came to pay their respects to the poor unfortunate man, who lost his life in the late eighteen hundreds at the hand of one of Thaddeus's men.

"I have to say, this is rather strange," Mary murmured, as she and the others went in to take their seats in the parlor.

"Yes, but the man deserves to have a proper burial after what the girl's father done to him," Jarred put in surprisingly.

"And Mom," Brenda leaned in to say, "we have all heard over the years about the hauntings that's been going on around here. Perhaps it will all come to an end someday. Besides, now we don't have to wonder what had happened to him."

"Yes, of course. But just supposing our other not so friendly spirit decides to show himself?"

"That won't happen until midnight," Ramsey murmured, just as he went to take a seat next to her.

"And Morgan? How has he taken to Thaddeus's ghost? Or should I say, how has Thaddeus taken to seeing Michael's look-a-like under the same roof?" she laughed.

"Not too well," he too laughed.

Being a strong devolved Catholic woman, it was quite astounding how Mary Ashford spoke of the dead. Though after years of hearing about the Morgan's Plantation hauntings, she had rather adapted to the theory of certain spirits inhabiting the place.

Meanwhile, up in his room getting ready, Morgan was just about to turn and look into the mirror to fix his tie, when Cynthia appeared with her hair all on top of her head in a loose bun, while wearing the same long white eighteen hundred's style gown, with its high laced neckline.

"You look lovely," he turned to say, while yet there was a little glimmer of Michael hiding in his eyes, wishing that he could hold her.

"You really think so?" she asked, while fighting to look directly at him.

"Yes."

Seeing how timid she was at the change, he reached out to take her hand, while wondering if with Michael being a part of him now, would make it possible to touch her.

"We should be getting downstairs," she cried, while pulling away, before he could make contact.

"Cynthia, what is it? Is it my being Michael now that bothers you?"

"No! No, o...o...of course not," she fibbed, having her back turned toward him.

"Oh...?" he whispered, as he came up behind her to place his arms lovingly around her small waist. The whole experience was quite new to him, but both Michael and Morgan wanted to hold their lost love, yet again. "Muffet..." Michael's more seductive voice came through, as she laid her head back against his chest, "please, don't be frightened, this is all so very new to me, as well! But just think of how we are now able to be together. If only..." he broke off, as she turned to face him with tears welling up in her eyes.

"If only father wouldn't come in between us?"

"Yes. It seems that as this Morgan and I bond as one, I'm learning quite a bit of what all has been going on since my..." he stopped to look away, when then she touched her delicate hand to his handsome face. As she did, she was able to feel the warmth, as he turned back to see her glistening eyes look into his.

"I love you, Michael," she cooed. "And as for Cat, she... No. I love you too, Morgan," she smiled tearfully, as he went to lightly trace his lips over hers.

Feeling the connection, he didn't stop there, but deepened his kiss to taste her lips all that much more, when then, there came a knock at the door, breaking up there soon to have been heated moment.

"Damn the house guests," he groaned, while holding her close in his arms, as her scent of lilac filled his nostrils.

"Morgan..." Nate called in through the closed door.

"Yeah. Coming!" he smiled down on her. "Are you ready?" he asked, before turning to the door.

"I will be right down. Though I am not all that sure that I will be able to..."

"Materialize all that long?"

"Yes. However, you, Ramsey, and Jarred will be able to see me now. As for the others, I don't know as of right now."

"As Cat, will Brenda ever see you, or her, I mean?"

"When the time is right, I will open up to her."

"Morgan?" Nate cut in once again.

Shaking his head, he quickly kissed her, as she began to laugh at their predicament.

Meanwhile, going on down to join the others, it wasn't long before a smile came over Jarred's face at seeing his little squirt come walking in. Though the smile changed just as she saw what was left of Michael's real body, as it lay skeletally in the casket.

Suddenly, as she began to feel lightheaded, as if that were possible, Morgan's friends cleared the room in record-breaking time so that he could go to her.

Sweeping her up into his arms, both Jarred and Nate were taken aback by what they saw, from the foyer, when he did so.

"I...I...I don't un...understand! How..." Jarred groaned, as the color went from his face.

"Ramsey, will you explain it to him?" Morgan asked, and then looking to his other friend, "Nate, I need to get her up to my room. Please..."

"All right. Just let me make sure the coast is clear."

Doing so, everyone was waiting out on the front porch, when he appeared, looking pale.

"Nate..." Mary spoke first, seeing his expression, "what is it? What just happened in there?"

"As you know," he lowered his voice, so not everyone would hear, "this whole thing was set up so Cynthia could see her lost love for the last time, before his remains were taken away."

"She fainted, didn't she?" Brenda asked.

"Yes, but there's more."

"What?" the two asked hastily.

"M...Morgan," he began shakenly. "He was able to physically pick her up."

"What...?" Jason cried out in a harsh-like whisper, when he came around after having overheard the last part of the conversation.

"I can't go into it now with the others here, but it's true."

"The Stable? What Ramsey was telling us? All that is true?"

Nodding his head, he turned to go back in after telling them to give him a minute. "I'll just go in and see how things are going," he offered.

Once inside, giving Morgan the go ahead, he was off on his way up to his room, while Ramsey was wrapping up on telling Jarred how it was possible for Morgan to do what he did. "Until their spirit becomes one with each other, Michael's will be able to react with hers, in every way possible."

"And Thaddeus?" Nate piped in. "Does this mean the two will be able to have a real knock down drag out fight, once they face one another?"

"Thaddeus may not know it at the time, but, yes."

"Good, God almighty, I wouldn't want to be here when that happens," Jarred put in ominously.

Hearing the front door open, they turned to see the others return.

"Excuse me, Sir," Brice began, "but it is getting late, and the boys are waiting to see Mr. Fairington to his new resting place."

"Sure," Nate replied, looking up the stairs toward Morgan's room, "I don't think it will

be a problem."

With the help of the others, no sooner had they gotten the casket taken out, and securely loaded, the two men left with barely no time to clear the driveway, when Scott came barreling in.

"What the..." Jarred growled, seeing his friend.

Going on out to see what the hurry was, Jason turned quickly to Nate, "What's going on?" he asked, while watching the front door, as well.

"It's Scott, one of Copeland's men. But not to worry, he's one of ours now, too. He probably has news from the front, as we call it."

"Copeland?" Jason repeated.

"Yes."

Going on out to see what was going on, the women stayed behind incase Morgan was to come back down.

Meanwhile, up in his room, lying in next to her, he carefully pulled out the stickpin that was holding her hair up, as she began to come to.

"Mmmm..." she murmured softly.

"Muffet...!" he called out. "Muffet... can you hear me?"

"M...Michael...?"

"Yes, my love, it is me."

"Mmmm... am I dreaming?"

"No, I'm afraid not."

"Oh, no_____! No_____!" she cried into his chest. Why_____? Why did he have to take you away from me_____?"

"He was afraid of losing you. Afraid as he was when your mother passed away."

"But he wouldn't have really...! Well, not until..."

"Until what?"

Telling him what Morgan had told her, his eyes grew dark and sad at the thought of having lost her then, as well.

"And Morgan's wife?"

"The same. Oh, Michael, I'm..." she began, as he went to place his fingers over her lips to stop her.

"I know you are, or were, his wife, as well."

"Does that upset you? Remember, at the time my spirit had gone in search of you. And when he and I met, well, it was as if I were looking right at you! And now..." She stopped to place her own fingers up to his lips.

Taking them into his hand, he kissed them tenderly one by one, until she couldn't take it any longer, when the two began to kiss once again. Only as time seemed to go on, so had their love, taking their essences to the limit and then some.

Soon, Morgan's clothes were laying in a heap on the floor nearby, as well as her own, and together, with the lights on, they clung to each other out of great need. As he drove his passion inside her, he felt her essence grow so much stronger, as each plunge grew more and more.

"Oh, M...Michael..." she whimpered out her ecstasy.

"Cynthia..."

Soon the passion came to a peak, when he drew back to study her expression, as he left her with all he could muster in such short time of being back. "Muffet, I love you, remember that."

"M...M...Michael_____!" she cried, as her eye flew open just then.

Seeing the fear etched in them, he smiled warmly, "No, my love, I'm not leaving you.

Not ever," he groaned, taking her back into his arms, as he went to roll over.

"Th...th...then... what...?"

"I have to rest up, as do you," he laughed boldly. "Muffet?" he then spoke softly.

"Yes?"

"You realize, we had made love with the lights on this time?"

"Uh huh...!" she replied, feeling her cheeks warming, as if she were blushing, while nuzzling even more into his arms. "And it no longer bothers me. Besides," she pulled away bravely to gaze upon him, "I love the way you look. And yes, even him."

"Because you are remembering having been this Catherine?"

"Yes."

Feeling their energy start to plummet, the two laid quietly in one another's arms, until she was gone to regain her own strength, as was he, leaving Morgan to lie sleeping as he was, until shortly before eleven, Nate and Jason came to check on him.

Hearing the knock, he slowly rolled out of bed to answer the door, having forgotten that he had nothing on.

"Well," Nate teased, "having a little rest, are we?"

Looking down as a cool breeze whist by made things a little unbearable, he grabbed for his robe and pulled it on. "Just give me a couple of minutes to get a hot shower and I will be right down. Oh, and do we have anything to eat?"

"Oh, and hungry, as well, are we?" Jason added grinningly, when Morgan opened the door the rest of the way to go across the hall to the bathroom, while carrying a fresh change of clothes that he had gotten off the back of a chair.

"Frankly, I am starving," he replied back at them, as he shook his head, while going on into the bathroom.

Hearing the water running, the two turned, laughing, as they headed back down the stairs.

"I gather you had gotten him up?" Ramsey asked, while standing in front of a nice warm fire that he had just built back up with Jarred and Scott's help, who had just gone back out to get some more to last the night and part of the next morning.

"Yes, it seems as though both Michael and Morgan have been reunited with their lost love," Jason teased.

"Oh, but it is Morgan who is up now," Ramsey smiled.

"Just how can you tell?" he asked puzzledly.

"By now the spirits of Michael and Cynthia are drained and need recharging. Who else can it be?"

"Well, whoever it is, he is starving. So what do you say we whip together some food? I know I could sure use a bite about now after all that has been going on around here," he added, on his way back to the kitchen, while the others followed.

Coming down shortly after his shower, Morgan was surprised to see Scott seated at the table. "What's going on?" he asked, walking in to take a cup of freshly brewed coffee from Ramsey.

"Scott came by earlier, just after the showing, to tell us about Copeland's plans to go after Jack Daniel and the mare," Nate offered, while fixing his friend up with a plate.

"Oh...? And how soon is this going down?"

"In less than two weeks," Scott replied. "He and his men are going out of town to work quietly on his own thoroughbred. He says, when he returns he wants the matter all taken care of."

"Like hell it will!" Jason yelled, as he nearly gave away his reason for being there.

"What?" Scott asked, not having been let in on why he was really there, but only told that he was to give Morgan a hand with the place, until he could get it up and running on his own.

"He's an animal lover, like the rest of us are," Morgan stated, while shaking his head, smiling.

Meantime, soon after they all finished eating, Ramsey looked up at the kitchen clock and then to Morgan.

Seeing the unspoken message on his face, Morgan knew the time was almost upon them. "Listen, guys! For those of you who know the story of Thaddeus Morgan, you are welcome to stay on. However, for those of you who don't, and value your sanity, might I suggest that you part company now, or forever take a strong sleeping pill. I have a feeling that tonight at midnight just might get a little rough for some of us," he teased lightly so as not to scare anyone.

"Hey, you can count on me to staying around to give you a hand," Jarred offered bravely.

"Yeah, me too," Jason spoke up prematurely, when the light began to flicker.

"Oh, oh..." Nate groaned. "I think we may be in for an early visit!"

"Ramsey...?" Morgan turned to see him going to the back door. "You're not leaving us now, are you?"

"No. Just letting Spooks in, is all."

Hearing the rattle of his tags, Morgan looked greatly relieved to see him. By then, the light really did start to flicker, as everyone at the table sat perfectly still.

"What do we do?" Nate asked worriedly.

Lighting a few candles, Ramsey turned just then to see an off white mist going into the den and then the parlor. Holding up a hand, he pointed to the back stairwell. "Go, now," he whispered to the others.

"But why?" Nate asked puzzledly.

"We must band together on this visit, as Michael isn't ready to face Thaddeus alone just yet."

"Great!" they all grumbled, while heading lightly up to the second floor, where right off, Spooks headed for Cynthia's room to look for her.

"Any signs, boy?" Morgan began to ask, when everyone turned to see movement coming up from the front stairs.

"Morgan, you didn't tell me that I would be doing something quite like this..." Jason quivered fearfully.

"Sorry, pal," he was saying, when suddenly his vision began to blur a little.

While trying to shake it off, Nate looked to him right away. "What is it, buddy? You don't look so well."

"I...I'm not seeing all that well..." He stopped, when he began to realize Michael was returning from his rest period.

"Morgan?" Jarred stepped forward, as Thaddeus appeared a few feet away from them.

Chapter Sixteen

"W h o   c a l l e d   m y   n a m e...?" Thaddeus asked, looking from one man to another. When he came to Morgan, Nate and Jarred stepped out in front of him. "Who are you? And why are you here, in my house?"

"We are here as guests of Morgan Fairbanks, husband to the late Catherine Habersham-Fairbanks," Nate answered bravely, without wavering one step away from his friend.

"Catherine Habersham-Fairbanks, did you say?"

"Yes," Ramsey replied, holding firm to his old, leather medicine pouch.

With Spooks staying by his master's side, Michael looked right into Thaddeus's eyes, bitterly.

Seeing this, Jarred quietly nudged him, "Hey, pal, you don't want to confront him yet. You're not ready."

"You know then, who I am?"

"Yes, I sort of figured it out when you began to look a little lightheaded there."

Just then, realizing it as well, the look Thaddeus gave Michael was heated.

Sensing it, Spooks came around to let himself be known.

"You again...?" Thaddeus growled.

"Yes, Thaddeus Morgan," Michael pushed passed his friends, "he is still here, and watching over Cynthia for me."

"For you...?" Jason and Nate turned in surprise; not realizing it was Michael, now.

"But I thought the dog..." Nate stopped.

"You thought right," Michael returned. "But Thaddeus hated the dog, for every time he would go anywhere near his daughter, the dog had thought he was going to hit her."

"I would have never hit my daughter," he growled. *"She was all I had after Constantina died. I loved her."*

"Enough to have me killed...?" Michael roared furiously. "And then the dog as well...?"

"And how would you have known that?" he asked.

"How else? You had him boarded up with me, until I sent him out to watch over the other Habersham women that followed. Although, I never knew about the bloody curse, which took their lives. That would explain your anger after finding out we were going to have our own baby. You feared she would be next to go. Did you know about the curse, as well?"

"No of course not. It was something that I had noticed whenever a Habersham woman had gotten pregnant. I...I thought that it was something in their bloodline. That is why I was so furious to hear about the baby. I had hoped that you would have just taken the money and left, before it had gone that far. Nevertheless, I was too late. By then, I was so angry at the two of you, I couldn't see straight."

"So you ordered his death...!" Jason spoke up in his official voice.

"Michael," Thaddeus choked back on his regret of what he had done to him, *"it wasn't what I had wanted to do. I loved you like a son!"*

"So I had thought," he shook his head sadly. "Why couldn't you have just trusted me enough to love her, and to have taken care of her_____?" he thundered. "Why_____?"

"Like I said_____ she was all I had_____!"

"And all I ever loved_____," Michael returned bitterly. "But you just had to take that away from me_____! You_____!" he growled. "Damn you_____!"

Seeing Thaddeus begin to waver, they didn't know what to expect next. But then he turned and disappeared.

"Is he gone?" Nate asked nervously.

"For now," Ramsey offered, turning to Michael, "but not for good."

"What?" the others asked.

"Michael had just given him reason to doubt what he had done to him."

"And now?" Michael asked.

"Now, he waits."

"For what?" they asked.

"To see how you are with his little girl. If she proves to be happy, he goes to join his wife once and for all."

"Well, I've heard enough," Jarred groaned.

"Same here," Nate agreed. "And if we are going to get these repairs done so we can get the horses over here, we had all better be getting some sleep. It's late as it is."

After saying their goodnights, knowing it was going to be peaceful from there on out, everyone chose a bedroom and went to it. Michael, though, headed to Cynthia's room first to see about her.

"Mor..."Jarred stopped and grinned. "Michael, I mean."

"No. Call me Morgan, since that is my name in this time."

"All right. If you were able to send the dog out, why didn't you just leave it too?"

"The dog wasn't killed there. I was. So it was able to travel wherever he wanted."

"But he chose to stay here?"

"Because of his mistress. And after she died, he returned to me. Although from time to time he did go out for a while. I suppose to watch over our daughter from what I have learned through Morgan."

"Yes, Constance, who was named after her grandmother in a way, you might say."

"I can understand that. That was how Cynthia would have wanted it."

At that, the two nodded their goodnights, and parted company. While down the hall in an adjoining room, Jason and Nate stayed up a little while longer to talk.

Hearing their muffled sounds, Michael smiled as he went on in to see his lady standing there, looking so proud as she ran into his arms to be held.

"Hey, yourself!" he grinned warmly.

"I was so... proud of you, just then."

"I just said what I felt. Though, I have to admit, having this extra piece of information sure did help."

"And now?" she asked, looking up into his caring eyes.

"We go back into the other room, where we were earlier."

"And what?" she asked mischievously.

"For me, sleep, little one. I want to be able to hold you in my arms all night long."

"Mmmm... I like the sound of that!" she cooed, while going along with him and their dog to his room, where Spooks had decided to curl up at the end of their bed, once again.

Waking the next morning, alone, Morgan got up and grabbed a quick shower, before heading out to get started on the last stable. Upon coming downstairs, he found Ramsey already in the kitchen working on breakfast for everyone.

"Good morning. How was your night?" the old Indian asked over his shoulder, while flipping the eggs.

"Peaceful," he smiled. "And yours?"

"Slept like a baby," he smiled back, while picking up a plate to hand him. "Toast and coffee are sitting out in the dining room. Thought with all of us here we ought to eat in there for a change. If that's all right with you?"

"Sure. That reminds me, I'll be looking for a full time cook and housekeeper starting tomorrow, if you know of anyone interested."

"Can't say that I do, but I'll be sure to pass it on," he returned, just as they heard another set of footsteps walking in just then.

"What's this about a cook and a housekeeper?" Jarred asked, while looking around for the coffee pot.

"Tomorrow, I will be taking interviews for the positions. So if you know of anyone, tell them to be here early."

"Coffee's in the dining room," Ramsey grinned, when seeing his bafflement at the scent, but no sign of a pot anywhere.

"Thanks," he returned, heading that way, but then stopped short of the doorway. "You know, Mom just might be interested in the cook's position."

"Good. Send her over," Morgan grinned. "And what about Brenda, would she be interest

ed in making some extra money, as well?"

"Heck, yes...!" he laughed, taking a heaping plate of food from Ramsey, when offered.

Seeing Nate come stumbling in next, Morgan teased, "Are we hungry, Nate?" he laughed, watching him go to ruffle his hair some.

"C...c...coffee," he uttered out. "W...w...where did you hide it?"

"Dining room," Jarred grinned. "Come on, I'm headed that way myself."

Looking to Ramsey, the two just grinned, shaking their heads.

"Better go and eat now, before it gets cold on you," Ramsey told Morgan, as he turned back to fix up the last two plates.

Seeing this, Morgan looked back on him puzzledly, "What's with just two more plates? Where is Jason this morning?"

"Already been down! He's now out seeing to the early morning delivery of the wood for the last stable!"

"Here? Already?"

"Sure is!"

"Boy they don't waste any time getting it here!"

"Nope. Many of the folks around here are might glad to see this place up and running again. Word has it, you might even consider giving old man Copeland a run for his money."

"What...? Who said that?"

"Just talk," he fibbed, having gotten the rumor going on his own.

"Hell, what do I know about thoroughbreds? As far as horses go, I just know how to saddle them up and ride them."

"That's pretty much all you need to know. Leave the rest to the trainer, herself!"

"*Her*...self? You want to explain just who this girl is, and how she came to being my trainer without so much as a word from me on this matter?"

"Her name is Jade Running Horse. My granddaughter. And she's a pro, since before the deaths of my youngest son and his wife, two years ago."

"Sorry, Ramsey. What happened?"

"Copeland's my guess. She trained Jack Daniel's Father to win. Aside from warnings to pull back, since he not only had the stallion put to death, but my family too."

Shaking his head, he got quite for a moment.

"Ramsey, what, if you don't mind my asking, happened to your family?"

"A car accident, out south of here. It was raining just after the race had ended."

"And?"

"Well, if truth be known!" He turned and looked squarely at Morgan. "I believe he was out to get my granddaughter, but something came up at the last minute.."

"Your son and his wife got it instead. But how?"

"They took the car, she was meant to be driving, and left her with the truck, since she was going to be hauling some supplies over to the clinic for me the next day." He turned away then to get them some silverware.

"Well, that explains why you hate the man so."

"Hate is such a strong word," he said sadly, while the two went on into the dining room.

After eating, the phone in the entryway sounded off, startling them.

"I'll get it," Morgan replied, getting to his feet.

"Just leave your plate, I'll see to it along with the others," Ramsey offered, while getting

up to get started on cleaning up.

With a nod of his head, he was out of the room, and into the foyer, before too many more rings could sound off. "Hello…" he answered deeply.

"Morgan?" Steve's voice sounded happy on the other end.

"Steve…?" he grinned excitedly.

"Yes. We got things all taken care of here, and are just about to head out. I just wanted to call and see how you're holding up, and to tell you that we are on our way."

He laughed, looking up to see Cynthia standing at the top of the staircase.

"What's so funny?" his friend asked.

"Oh… nothing, really. I'm just fine," he grinned. "The guys are all here. Not to mention, a few more hands than what I had started out with. Were you guys still planning on staying with Nate when you get in?"

"That was the plan! Why?"

"Well, the plans have changed."

"What…?"

"Yes. Nate and Jason have been staying out here with me."

"But what of this ghost thing?"

"Not a problem," Morgan laughed again. "We'll tell you all about it when you guys get here. Now, just when will that be?"

"How is tomorrow, about this time? Christy wants to drive on through, changing off every so often."

"Can you do that with two U-Hauls and three vehicles?"

"Sure! When she is driving, I will be sleeping, and so on."

"Oh, then what am I missing here? Who is driving the U-Hauls, and who is driving the vehicles? Because I really would like to have mine here, when you get here."

"That's what we are driving, along with a large, enclosed trailer with our more important things. Like your living room, bedroom, and utility room things. As for the clothes, they are with the trucks that we hired to have driven down. They should be arriving right around the time we get there. Which reminds me. Where do you want them to deliver it?"

"Here. Yours too. With what you have with you, we'll put my things here in the house, since I still have plenty of room. I'll just have the guys to hold off on the repairs long enough to move the things in the parlor, into the den so my living room furniture can go in the parlor."

"And our things?"

"What stuff of yours that you will have with you, we will put it here in the house for the time being. The rooms upstairs are pretty big and plentiful. What we don't get up there, we can put out in the first stable. It's pretty clean, and safe to store both our things in. Trust me on that, I know," he laughed.

"And the other things that are coming on the trucks?" Steve asked. "The stable, as well?"

"Yes. And just as soon as I get off here, I'll talk to Nate and see what we can line up in the way of a house for you guys. Something close to one of us, so you won't have to keep your things out in the stable too long. Which brings me to ask, what sort of house are you wanting?"

"Something not quite as large as yours, but more like Nate, for when we have company, we will have plenty of room to put them."

"Great! I know just the one. Right up from Nate's place is a house with your name written all over it," he roared. "In fact it's a smaller image of mine, with a huge backyard with an in ground pool and garden space, which you all will love."

"And the price?"

"A little up there, but if I know you, you'll get them to bring it down some. And not too far from there is Nate's old practice, until you find something more to your liking."

"Well if the house is all that you say it is, we'll have to stay where Nate's old practice is for awhile. Besides, that clinic wasn't all that bad to begin with. We'll be fine there. Maybe even do some work on it to spruce it up some. Isn't it over by the animal hospital he's at now?"

"Yes. Right across from it, in fact."

"Great! Then it all settled. Call the realtor and set up a time for us to see the house, and afterwards we will go and see this old clinic of his."

"That shouldn't be too difficult, he's been renting it out to another doctor, friend of his that I haven't met yet," he explained, when turning to see Nate standing there.

"Good. We can hardly wait to see you guys. Oh, but wait!"

"What?"

"What about the your vehicles?"

"They are being pulled behind the two large U-Hauls."

"Good thinking. Hey, tell the two I said hello. And Steve?"

"Yeah?"

"Be careful driving down."

"Yes, mother dearest," he laughed, and hung up.

Turning back, Morgan came face to face with Jarred as well, after they gave Ramsey a hand carrying in their dishes.

"Was that you guy's friend, Steve?" he asked.

Grinning, "Yep! They'll be in about this time tomorrow. And... I have extended out an invitation for them to stay here, too. You both will be staying too of course, won't you? Since

I have already told him you are." He turned to address Nate, smiling.

"Yeah, sure…! I suppose I could. After all, how often does one get to stay in a Haunted Plantation, with a man who has an extra spirit living inside him? Not to mention, a beautiful one to sleep with?" he laughed.

"How did you know about that?" Morgan asked.

"I got up to check on you. You know, the doctor in me and all?" he smiled.

"So, you saw her, did you?"

"Yes, and your alter ego, Michael. Now, as for Steve and the others, what are we going to tell them, when they get here? And what about the house down the street from mine?"

"Tell them the truth!" he continued grinning.

"Yeah, right," Jarred laughed. "I can see it now. *New owner of plantation gets locked away for having a split personality.*"

He laughed, as well, "Yes well, that part of course will have to be told delicately. Still it has to be told just the same. As for the house, call the realtor and see about setting up a time to see it tomorrow evening, sometime. And see if they will come down on the price. I told Steve it was up there, but I have no idea if it is or not. It just looks like it would be with the size of yard it has, and the pool I got a glance of, when we were living the other day."

"All right, but first I am going up to get a shower out of the way, so we can get started on the work at hand. I want to get Jack Daniels and his mom brought over, while Copeland and his goons are out, from what Scott told us the other night when you, or I should say, Michael went on upstairs with his lady love," Nate grinned along with Jarred.

"Fine. See you two out at the stable just as soon as you are through," he returned, while heading for the kitchen, to go out the back way. "Oh, and don't forget to call that realtor!" he called back, on his way out. "Steve is counting on us to help get them settled in!"

"I'll do that!" Nate called back after him, while turning to head up the stairs with Jarred.

"Buddy, you might want to do that now, before it slips you mind," he suggested.

"Yes, but to do that, I will have to call information to get the number first."

"No you won't! Mom has it. She has been cleaning for the company for some time now. I'll just call her and get the number for you."

Doing that, before too long, Nate had the time set up, along with some pertinent information on the place, and the shower all out of the way.

Meanwhile, down at the third stable, Jason was up to his wits end with paperwork, while waiting on extra men to be sent by the New Orleans Police Department.

"Sir...!" one of the delivery guys called out. "Where would you want these rolls of fencing to be put?"

"Over by the corral for now," he instructed, when hearing a vehicle pull up.

Getting out, Morgan scanned over the area, while pulling out his tool belt. Seeing the trucks parked every which way, shaking his head, he called out to his friend, "Jason."

"Yeah."

Waving a hand over the area, he commented, "We are going to have a mess on our hands when they get ready to pull out."

Seeing what he was referring to, Jason yelled to one of the burly, guys that were about to climb up into one of the one-ton trucks to leave, "George...!" he circled his arm around in the air. "Move it up, and then back in beside the stable. You'll be able to get out better that way."

Waving a hand, the man got in and did as he was told.

"Well, what do you think?" Jason asked, turning back to his friend.

"Looks like we have got our work cut out for us. Now, if we only had a few more hands."

"They're on the way."

"What?"

"The Commander is sending out four guys for now to act as stable hands. Then later, a few more."

"Can they be trusted though? How do we know who Copeland has in his back pocket, and who he doesn't?"

"Jarred gave me a list last night to go over. If they are on the list, I will tell him no. He will know what I'm saying without leaking out the wrong bit of information over the phone."

"Good. Oh, and by the way, Steve and the others are on their way, as we speak."

"So soon? I would have thought..."

"Yes, me too, but he says everything is taken care of."

"Great! And where are they staying until they get settled in?"

"Here!" he smiled, knowing what Jason was going to say next.

"H...h...here...? With all that has taken place already?"

"Yep! And yes, we are going to tell them everything."

"E...e...every..."

"Thing," Morgan finished, while going over to have a look at the blueprints for the stables, and the ones for improving the bunkhouse. "Now, where are we on fixing up the stable?"

"From what I can see," Jason went on, while pointing out the doors and windows, and what few boards needed replacing, the day went by without a hitch.

Chapter Seventeen

That evening, after checking on the first stable for their things to go in, getting the parlor switched over to the den, the others sat around a bon fire, set off by using the old wood from the second and third stable.

As for Morgan, it was Michael, now, who went in to find Cynthia looking all so teary-eyed out the parlor window. "Hey there, why so unhappy?" he asked, walking in all sweaty and dirty from the long day's work.

"I haven't been out in such a long time!" she sniffled quietly, as he went up to place his arms around her waist from behind.

"Afraid that you may not be able to go outside the perimeter of these walls?"

"Y...yes...!"

"Give me a couple of minutes to grab a quick shower, and I'll be right down to take you out."

"But, what if I..."

"No. You won't. Your death wasn't like mine. So you should be able to walk out those doors," he pointed to the front hall, "whenever you want to. But for the first time, I want to be the one taking you out, in case there is a problem."

Tuning into his arms, she smiled up at him

"Wait for me," he smiled back, kissing her nose. "I'll be right down. You hear me? Don't go anywhere. Particularly out there," he gestured, looking out the window.

"I will wait," she promised.

And wait, she did, while he hurried up to his room to get out a clean pair of jeans, socks, and a v-neck sweater, since it was getting cool out.

Rushing off to get his quick shower, he was back downstairs in no time, straightening his sweater on his way down the stairs. "Ready?" he called out, grabbing his denim jacket off the hall tree, when he had already decided where they were going to walk.

"Yes," she said, appearing in the foyer, looking excited.

Smiling down on her, he took her hand and headed for the front doors. The first few steps out through the grand doors were rather scary for her, when she felt the air on her face for the first time, since Catherine's death, a little over three weeks ago.

"Are you all right?" he asked, taking her close into his arms.

"Oh... yes...! It's so beautiful out here," she cooed excitedly.

"Shall we go for that walk now?"

"Where to...?" she asked, looking up to see his smiling face.

Not saying anything, she knew right off, when they headed out across the side yard, and through a few old forgotten rose gardens, one right after another, until they reached a broken area in the split rail fence. To one side of it was an old metal bucket hanging off two fence posts. In it were old daises grown from the previous year. As for the rest of the fence, it stretched out as far as the eye could see.

And then, there it was. Off to one side of the field was an old stone carriage house that he used over a hundred years ago.

The same one, which their daughter, Constance was conceived from their love.

"Oh, Michael..."

"You remember it?"

"How could I not? Had it not been for the horrible rain that day, we would have not been out here."

"I know. I was just coming in from seeing to the horses, when I glanced up to see you out picking those daisies. Lord, girl, your white dress was a mess, and that so called hat you were wearing."

"It too was a mess," she laughed lightly. "Now what do we do? It isn't raining, and..." she began, only to be cut off by his kiss, when he swept her around to claim her lips.

"Let me be the one to decide that," he groaned, wantingly.

Looking around them, he saw off in the far distance the flicker of flames from the bon fire, and heard the muffled sounds of men's voices. Taking her hand, he led her over to a low spot in the fence to cross over. At which, he picked her up in his arms, and soon had her on the other side, before crossing over himself.

"Let's go inside and see how it looks," he suggested, leading the way, once again.

No sooner had they pushed open the door with a little force of his shoulder, the two saw all the dust and cobwebs looming around them.

"It's so dirty in here," she cried, with a slight shiver to her voice.

"Cold?" he asked, looking down at her.

"I...I shouldn't be...! I didn't think I could feel this way."

"Well, not for long," he offered, while giving her his jacket, before going around to straighten up the place.

"Wait... silly!" she laughed.

"What...?" Looking at her, and then the jacket, he realized his error, and laughed. "You can't wear it like this, huh?"

"Uh huh!" She shook her head sweetly.

"Well," he smiled, "I guess I'll just have to get a fire going, huh?"

It wasn't long before the place was as it had been all those years ago. Even the warm fire, crackling in the stone fireplace, at the far end of the living room still held its charm.

"Oh, Michael," she cried happily, while looking around the beautifully lit room, with all its warm earth-tone colored furniture uncovered by the white sheets that protected them, "it's as if time has repeated itself."

"Perhaps it has," he replied, with a smile, while standing by the fireplace.

"But we know better." She turned, looking at him.

"For now," he came walking up to her, "let's just hold onto what we have," he returned, while taking her hand back into his, to lead her over to the couch.

"Michael, what are you up to?" she asked, when he gestured for her to take a seat.

"Wait and see," he replied, mischievously, while reaching down into his pocket to pull out the ring Morgan had slipped into it earlier. Afterwards, going down on one bended knee, he took her hand in his, once again, as a smile lit his handsome face, causing his eyes to sparkle. "Miss Morgan, I had planned on giving you this ring the following day, but..." He hesitated, when the memory of what had taken place that night crept in.

Seeing this, she cried, "Oh, Michael, please don't go back there," she sadly begged.

"No. You're right."

Looking into her tear-filled eyes, he started over again. Though, when it came time to slipping on the ring, or at least show it to her, she cried, when catching sight of its glistening stone by the firelight.

"Will you... marry me?" he finished, with such warmth radiating from his beautiful green eyes.

"M...marry you? But, how...?" she cried.

"I'll have to work on that. Though in the eyes of God, even if we had one of their friends contact..." He stopped.

"Michael...?"

"What am I thinking?" he laughed. "Ramsey can do it."

"Well, yes, of course," she smiled sweetly, "since he already knows of us!"

"We can have him officiate the ceremony, while the others who know about us can be there, too. Oh, and there will be three more about to join us soon."

"Oh?" she asked, getting up puzzledly. "Who?"

"Catherine's doctor, Steve, and his family."

"They will be staying on up at the house?" she went on fearfully, while pacing the floor. "But what of daddy? What if he were to show up? They will be terrified!" She stopped, when he stood, cutting off her path.

"No," he explained, when taking her gently by the arms, "he won't hurt them. He has changed somehow."

"Changed...? Daddy?"

"Yes. Last night, we talked. All of us, that is. And Ramsey seems to think that he's going

to stay quiet for the time being, to see what comes of you and I. And if I can prove that you're going to be happy, he will leave us be."

"If only he would."

"He will. He loves you. And he knows that I do too! So now, as to the answer to my question, will you marry me?"

"I have waited over a hundred years to hear you say those words."

"What's a hundred more?" he teased.

"No, silly! Of course I will marry you, and have your..." She abruptly stopped, and turned away, as the memory of their child, both his and Morgan's flashed by.

"Muffet, don't do this to yourself. That was then, and now is now. We have to go on."

"But our baby. It's not something that I can simply forget."

"I know, and Lord help me if only we could..." Suddenly he stopped, when recalling something Morgan had been told.

"Michael..." She turned back to see something come over him, just then. "What?"

"Cynthia, if you could come back. Would you want to?"

"Michael, where are you going with this? There are no other Habersham women out there. Catherine was it for me."

"Maybe as for the Habersham women go. But what if..."

"Another woman was to have gotten into an accident, and her spirit didn't want to go on any longer?"

"Would you?"

"I...I don't know...! It's just too hard to grasp right now. And what's the likelihood of that happening anytime soon?"

"I don't know, but Morgan's friend, Steve is a doctor, and if that were to happen, he could tell us."

"But Morgan is too!"

"Yes, in a sense, but he doesn't want to go back to that."

"So we wait on this Steve to tell him. And then what?" she cried.

"We could start our lives over again. And Lord, yes, have those wonderful babies to continue your father's plantation, when we're too old and gray to go on," he laughed, holding her close.

Seeing his joy, she too felt the hope fill her heart. "Until then, we wait to be married," she murmured lovingly against his chest.

"Fine." He pulled back to study her. "But as for this ring?"

"I can't physically wear it now, but when the time comes..."

"And it will, my love," he smiled warmly, while slipping the ring back into his pocket, where later he would place it on a chain to be worn around his neck, until he could place it on her finger. "I love you."

"And I love you," she cried, as he went on to hold her dearly.

Chapter Eighteen

After a while of talking over what all had been happening, the two got up to head for the door, then stopped to look back on their warm fire, as it was nearly out.

"I should extinguish it before leaving. I would hate it if this place were to burn down."

"Me too," she murmured, while standing poised in the doorway, while he went out to find some rain water sitting in an old bucket.

Getting it taken care of, they set off for the main house, where the others were now sitting around the parlor going over the next day's itinerary.

"Well, there he is?" Nate teased, seeing how their friend was smiling, as he walked in with his woman visible only to himself. "Where have you been?"

"Just out walking!" he smiled, while looking at Cynthia out of the corner of his eye.

"Just out walking, huh?" they smiled, sensing he wasn't alone, when they each looked down to see his hand, as if it had a hold of something.

"Yeah, there could only be one thing you would be holding onto there, buddy," Nate indicated with a nod of his head, down at his hand.

Morgan, and then again, Michael, just smiled, and headed on up to his room to be alone with her.

"Michael," she whispered, "why don't you go on back down and be with them awhile. I will be all right here waiting for you!"

"Nothing doing. You are just about out of energy, and I don't know how much longer it will be before Morgan and I are totally fused. For now, I just want to be with you. Can you handle that?"

"Then what did you have in mind?"

"This," he groaned, closing the door behind them, before taking her over to his bed. "I have wanted to make love to you ever since we had gotten out to the old carriage house, but too afraid we would have drained ourselves, before getting back here."

"Is that all you can think of?" she laughed.

"Well... no!"

"Good. Then what's stopping you now?" she teased.

"Not a damn thing," he groaned, while removing his things, before going on to hers.

"Not... a damn thing," he repeated, while taking her again into the night.

The next day, unaware he had overslept; Morgan woke, feeling utterly drained. "Oh..." he groaned, rolling onto his back. At that time, he looked around to see the mess his alter ego had made of the bed, as well as his clothes being tossed in the corner. Smiling, he slowly got up to strip the bed, before heading over to grab a shower, in hopes it would revitalize him so he could get started on the work that needed to be done that day.

Before he could get too far, there came a knock at his door.

"Morgan?" Nate called out from the other side, while smiling to himself.

Throwing on a pair of sweatpants found at the end of his bed, Morgan went to answer the door.

"Good morning. Did you sleep all right last night?" he asked, seeing the heap of linen lying at the end of the bed.

"Well you sure can't tell by the look of things, can you?" he smiled back at the mess, before passing his friend in the doorway, to head on over and get his shower out of the way.

Looking back into the room, Nate grinned, "No, you sure can't. Oh, and by the way," he turned to follow his friend, "Ramsey just sent me up to see if you were still coming down for breakfast."

"Yes. Just let me get washed up first."

"Yes, well, you best be pushing it. It's already after ten."

"What...?" he nearly yelled, coming back out of the bathroom. "But I had all those interviews to do this morning, and Steve and the others will be here at any time now."

"Yeah, well as for the interviews," Nate went on, while Morgan hurried back in to get his shower over with, "they were all a bust, knowing about the history of this place. Oh, but not all is lost, Mary and Brenda, chose not to let it get to them."

"They're here? Now?" he called out over the sound of running water.

"Yep! And lucky for you, I had Brenda start downstairs so she wouldn't walk in and see you and all your glory," he laughed.

"Yes, well that would have been quite a surprise for the both of us," he agreed, coming back out, while toweling off his wet hair.

"Oh, yeah, indeed," he continued to laugh, while Morgan crossed the hall naked, to go back into his room to dress.

"Nate?" he called out.

"Yes?"

"Let Ramsey know I'll be down soon."

"Sure thing," he said, turning to go, when leaving out that Steve and the others had already arrived.

Downstairs, having been told the story of what had been going on, down to Michael's spirit, Steve asked, when seeing Nate walk back in, grinning, "Why the amused look?"

"Morgan," Nate laughed. "The guy is a total mess this morning."

"Is he coming down soon?" Christy asked, while they went into the dining room to wait on him there.

However, their wait wasn't long. While Ramsey brought in a few plates of food for his friends, Nate was telling them about the house and clinic, right down to the asking price, for both, seeing how he had never told anyone that the clinic was his to begin with.

Walking in, Morgan still looked gray with fatigue. "Thanks, Ramsey," he said, taking his plate, while not seeing Steve standing off behind him. Turning, he nearly dropped his plate, as it hit the table with a clatter, when he finally noticed. "Steve_____" he cried happily, while going up to embrace his friend. "When did you guys get in?"

"Just before Nate went up to get you. So, is it true? This woman's spirit, and now her lost love to boot?"

"Is he really a part of you now, Uncle Morgan?" Lacy too asked, but sadly.

"Yes, Squirt, he is," he offered, while going over to give her a hug as well.

Though before he could, she pulled back.

"What is it?" he asked, sensing her apprehension.

"How will I know who I'm talking to? Are you my uncle, or this Michael, guy?"

"I am your uncle through and through, kiddo," he smiled, while taking her into his arms.

"And even if it were Michael, he is cool too, just like me," he teased. "We are even identical in how we look, just like your aunt Cat and Cynthia are."

"Then it's really true about Cat?" Christy asked. "She and Cynthia are one of the same?"

162

"Yes, and because she hadn't gotten the chance to full fill what the others had had, her... Cat's spirit reverted back to Cynthia."

"Then I'm glad to see how happy you really are," she cried, while going on tiptoes to give him a hug, before taking their seats.

At that time, Morgan went on to tell them more, while Ramsey brought in another plate for Steve.

"So you say this house is not as high priced as you had thought?" Steve asked, taking a bite of his food.

"No," Morgan explained. "From what Nate told me yesterday, while out at the stables, the owner is anxious to sell so they can move to Montana, where they have some land to raise horses on."

"And the clinic, you're only wanting twenty-five hundred a month to start out?" Steve asked Nate.

"Yes, while the others pay four times that," he grinned. "After all you guys are my closest friends. So why charge you more, when you haven't had time to get things set up and going well, yet?"

"Well, I certainly appreciate that!" he laughed. "Christy, what do you and Lacy think about all this?"

"I just want to see the house and pool," their daughter chimed in, excitedly.

"Christy?" he turned, hopefully.

"Honey, you know how I feel about working alongside you at the clinic, but I have to say..." she turned, looking to her daughter, and smiled, "I'm with Lacy on this," she laughed along with the others just then.

"Well, it's settled," Morgan grinned. "First thing after breakfast, we get the stuff unloaded that's going in here, and take what is mine that doesn't stay for now, on out to the stable to store, until I have time to look through it all."

"And our things," Steve turned, smiling, "we'll do the same as for what is in your Tahoe and on the trailer. The truck with our things can stay loaded for another day or two, until we know about this house we are going to see later this evening."

"Sounds good. As for what to do until then, after showing you around the place, can I get you guys' help on the stables? We have some very important horses coming soon that need caring for. And we need to be getting it down soon, if we are to be ready for them."

"Horses...?" Lacy cried excitedly, "Yes, sure...! I'm not afraid of a little dirt!"

"Count us in too," Christy added, looking to her husband.

"Yes, same here. However, we watch the time, so we can be cleaned up, to see this house and clinic of yours, Nate. I'm anxious to get things started once we get settled in, that is."

After breakfast was over, they went on the grand tour, and then got started on unloading their things, when the two U-Hauls arrived.

"Dad...!" Lacy called out from the front of the house, when seeing the trucks turn into the long driveway. "Dad! They're here!" she called again, when running around to the side of the house to tell him.

"So I see!" he returned, looking around him.

"What?" Morgan asked, seeing his confusion.

"Your things. You are going to have to tell them where you want your thing. Unless of course you still want them to go into the first stable, seeing how you still have a little more room in the house for them."

"No. In the stable they will go. I still have work to do on the house before I'm ready to put everything in there."

And in the stable they went, when soon after, everyone got started on what they could of the work needed to get things ready for the horses arrival.

A short while later, Ramsey came out with a young woman at his side. Fairly tall, like himself, she was beautifully shaped in her denim jeans, and buttoned down blue plaid shirt. "Morgan," he called out, walking up with his granddaughter on his arm. "This is Jade Ramsey, my granddaughter, who I refer to as Running Horse. A name, which she has been well deserved of in her field of work."

"Jade," Morgan smiled, while extending his hand out to the woman with long, flowing, blonde hair, and glistening blue eyes, unlike any Indian he had ever seen. Until something about them caught his attention. *'Something in the way of pain, but from what, and why?'* he wondered, while still having a hold of her hand.

"I take it you are to be my new boss?" she asked, determinedly.

"Yes. Yes, of course," he replied, when finally tearing himself away from those eyes of hers. "As for where you will be staying..." he began, when she cut him off.

"I have been staying with my grandfather. However, with him being out here so much, I suppose I can stay out in the bunkhouse with the others."

"No. I won't be having that," he refused.

"You, what...?" she glared up at him seethingly.

"You heard me. I won't be having no lady staying on in the same bunkhouse as the men!"

"I may be a lady to some extent," she informed him, with hands resting firmly on her hips, "but staying where I wish is my business. And as long as they leave me alone, I will do the same."

"Is that how you feel?" he glared back. "Well if it's the bunkhouse you want, it's sure as hell the bunkhouse you will get. But only if I have a room added on for you. Oh, and Miss Ramsey, is it? Here on my plantation you do as I tell you. You got that?"

"Fine," she returned heatedly, while he looked back to see Jason and a few of his men cleaning the place out, while trying not to eavesdrop on their conversation.

"Jason...?" Morgan called out, angrily.

Hearing his tone of voice, he dropped everything to see what he needed.

"Yeah, what is it?" he asked, running up.

"Miss Ramsey here insists on staying in the bunkhouse with the rest of you men when it is finished. So I need to have the guys start right away on adding a room to it, as well as another bathroom."

"Sure!" he said, looking to the woman who looked as if she could do some serious impair her new boss for being so chauvinistic. "Yeah... sure, I'll get right on it," he smiled.

"Jason...!" Morgan growled.

"You know what I mean," he corrected, sheepishly.

"Well... get started."

"Sure...!" Turning to leave, he heard her comment on wanting to help build it herself.

Grinning even more, he knew his friend had a mean one there to tend with, as he continued on back to fill the others in.

"Are you always this bullheaded, Miss Ramsey?" he asked.

"Only when a pale face like you tells me where I can and cannot stay. Now, if you will excuse me, I have work to do."

"Fine. You can just start with working on your own room addition," he growled, while taking off his own tool belt to offer it to her. Normally, as a gentleman, he would have adjusted the size to accommodate her. But in her case, he chose not to, as she went to put it on.

Seeing its loose fit, as it hung casually around her hips, he grinned silently, and turned back to Ramsey, as she went off toward the bunkhouse. "Your granddaughter, huh? Just where does she get that temper of hers?"

"From her mother, along with her hair and eyes," he commented, seeing how Morgan was looking into them earlier.

"Huh, and the look in her eyes? Is that from her temperament, or was there something in her life that would radiate such pain?" he asked, having forgotten about the woman's loss.

"She is still angry over what had happened to her parents."

"Damn, I'm sorry. I had almost forgot about that."

Watching her from a distance, he shook his head sadly and went on about what he was doing, before the interruption.

After a few more hours of blood, sweat, tears, and practical jokes, they heard the dinner bell ringing to call everyone in to eat.

"Let's hit it...!" Morgan called out, hanging up his hammer.

"Boy, I'm starving," Lacy cried, while running up to join her parents.

"Honey, I think we all are," Christy agreed, putting an arm around her shoulder.

"Yes. And the sooner we get done, the sooner we can get started on finishing the bunkhouse, now that the stable is nearly through. All but you three. Nate is going to have you follow him over to the house and clinic, while I finish up on a few more things around here," Morgan was saying, when suddenly an enormous weight came over him.

"Hey, buddy," Steve turned just then to see the look come over his friends' face, "what is it?"

"I...I really don't know!" he replied, while stopping to clear his head, before going on. Even then, the pressure he was feeling was growingly difficult to ignore, when Ramsey and Nate walked up to join them.

"Problem?" Nate asked, concernly, when going up to look his friend over in a more professional way. At that moment, seeing his color begin to drain from his face, he grabbed Morgan's arm and put it around his shoulder. "Jarred, give me a hand," he called out, as his friend began to waver.

Running up, Jarred grabbed the other arm. "Let's go buddy," he suggested, "we've got to get you back up to your room."

"Wh...what's happening to me?" he asked on their way back.

"I don't rightly know," Nate returned, "but it may have something to do with this fusion between you and Michael."

"Is it..." he began, as his head started to ache. "Is it happening now?"

"Quite possible," Ramsey suggested, while keeping up with them.

"Oh, God, please tell me this doesn't mean I won't be able to hold her again," he cried, not seeing the look that had just come over Jade's face, when having been told of the story of Cynthia and Michael years ago. And now to learn about Morgan's connection to the woman and her lost love?

"I'm afraid that's highly possible," Ramsey said regretfully.

"No...! I can't lose her again."

"You won't lose her, Morgan," Nate offered, while trying to sound positive.

"No, you just won't be able to feel her, is all," Jarred returned sadly.

"No_____!" he wailed, shaking his head. "No_____ I...I can't go through this again. Not now, don't you all see_____?" He pulled back. "I need her. Oh, God, I need her!"

Just as they reached his room to lie him down, Steve turned to his wife.

"I'll get it ready for you," she offered, knowing just what he would be needing, when she left the room to prepare a syringe with just enough sedative to help relax him.

"Take it easy, buddy," Steve murmured. "I'm going to give you something to help relax you."

"No, I just want to be with her!" he cried.

"Daddy...?" Lacy looked to her father frightenedly.

"I know, honey, it hurts me too to see him this way," he cried, holding her, while Nate and Ramsey looked him over.

Realizing something Ramsey saw in his eyes, he announced, "It's not Morgan talking. It's Michael, and he needs to be alone right now with his love," he explained, pulling back, while taking Nate with him.

"Grandfather," Jade spoke up, going with him. "Is this what you have been telling me about?"

"Yes. It seems as though the fusion is nearing its final steps now. The two will soon only be one."

"Already?" Nate asked.

"Yes. Michael will know everything there is to know about Morgan, and Morgan about Michael."

"But who will be who?" Lacy asked first, just as her mother returned with the syringe.

"They will be one of the same! Although, we will be calling him Morgan, as that is who he is in this time frame," Ramsey offered the twelve year old, kindly.

"Morgan," Steve came forward to pull his sleeve back, "you're going to feel a little sting. Try not to fight it. All right, pal?"

"But I'm not Morgan...! I'm..." he started, when the needle penetrated his skin. "M...Mi...chael..."

"I know you are," he replied sadly. "I know you are."

After giving him his shot, everyone took their leave, while Michael lay crying over the loss of being able to have Cynthia in his arms again. But just as he did, she appeared hovering over him.

"Please..." he cried out to her.

Saying no more, she went to him, as he held out his arms to her for the last time.

"I...I...I know," she too cried, holding him for as long as they could, until he rolled her over to claim her lips passionately, while not wanting to lose any more time with her.

Feeling it though, she clung to him that much more, as the kiss grew on.

When they stopped, he held her dearly. "We will still have our walks in the meadow," he told her, "and those quiet nights out at the carriage house. None of that will ever stop."

"No, of course not. And I will always be here with you, even as you sleep, if only to hear you breathe."

"Muffet..." he cried, touching her soft silky-like hair one last time. "I...I... I...love you!"

"And I, you, my darling. And I, you," she cried, kissing him again, but only to feel the electricity it had caused.

Meanwhile, giving Michael and Cynthia some time alone, Nate took Steve and his family on over to see the house and clinic, while not planning to stay away too long. As for Jason and Jarred, they used this time to get better acquainted, while keeping an eye on what was going on upstairs. Ramsey and his granddaughter, in the meantime, going for a walk to talk about what was going on, coming to the second stable, they went in to talk, when she announced about a vision she had had of her parents.

"Oh, Running Horse," he smiled sadly at her, before going over to fiddle with a latch on one of the stall doors, "it is only natural that you would be having these visions."

"But grandfather, you too?" she asked, not knowing how something was troubling him, then.

"Yes," he sighed painfully, "I too have been having them."

"But why...? Why are they are calling me? And worse yet, I want to go to them."

"Ah, yes, quite similar to my vision, as well!"

"They are calling out to you too?" she cried sadly.

"No. My son is trying to tell me you will be leaving me soon. But I don't know why!"

"I do." She turned quietly to walk away.

"You...?" He turned to study her with the same look of sadness in eyes, as he had when he walked away to fiddle with the latch on the stall door.

As his favorite granddaughter, he had spent many nights teaching her the Indian rituals, and how to listen to her own spirit, as it would tell her many things. Now, seeing it in her eyes, as she turned back to him, he knew her journey was about to meet its end. But how and when, he did not know.

"Grandfather, you know what I say is true. You taught me well."

"Yes, but I only wish that it weren't quite so true. I will miss you greatly, little one."

"And I will you," she smiled sadly.

Chapter Nineteen

Later that night, coming downstairs, after getting back from the clinic with a list of what they will be needing, Steve and the others went into the parlor and sat down to talk about it.

"How's Morgan?" he was asking, while getting comfortable.

"He's been quiet the whole time you guys have been gone," Jason replied, while taking a seat across from him, on the same color brown leather sofa, they were sitting on, being that there was a love seat to match, along with a recliner, an overstuffed chair, and a half dozen end tables, and a few lamps to accommodate them.

Hearing their voices from upstairs, Morgan came down to join them. When reaching the doorway, everyone looked up to see his tear-dampened face looking back at them.

"Uncle Morgan...?" Lacy unfolded her long legs to get up and go to him.

"Yes, it's me, sweetie," he returned, reaching out to her, as she ran up, throwing herself into his arms.

"How are you holding up?" the others asked, joining him.

"Like hell," he returned, while going in to have a seat with their help.

"The sedative should be wearing off soon," Christy offered thoughtfully. "Would you like some hot tea to help sooth what's ailing you?"

"Yes, sure."

"Uncle Morgan...?" Lacy looked worried.

"Yes?"

"M...Michael, where is he?"

"Here, just as I am."

"But..."

"We no longer have a divided spirit. It feels like there's only one of us here now."

"Just exactly how *does* that feel?" Steve asked, while sitting forward on one of the sofas.

"Like nothing has really happened! Oh, sure, I have more knowledge about being a..."

"Vet?" Nate laughed.

Shaking his head humorously, Morgan laughed too, "Yes... a gosh darn vet."

"Good! Now maybe we can really get down to some real work?" he carried on laughing, along with everyone else in the room.

"Yes, well that can wait until tomorrow," Christy stated, when coming back in with his tea. "First we want to fill you in about the house and clinic, if you are up to it."

"Yes, of course!" He brightened up some at seeing the look of joy on their faces. "How did that all go, anyway? Did you like the house and ground? And what about the clinic? Though, I know it could use your own personal touch."

"Well, for starters, the house and ground are amazing," Christy cried out, before her family could. "Oh, and of course that means having to go shopping for a few more bedroom sets. And Steve..." she smiled at the man, "is in heaven with the den that house has."

"That good, huh?" Jason laughed.

"Good...? It is incredible. And they said we can put our things into the three-car garage until the place is ready to move into. Anyway, enough of that. The clinic, like you said, needs some work, but it perfect, right where it is."

"Good. So does this mean you will be staying there?" Morgan asked, getting up to get a fire going.

"Yes," he smiled, while getting up to give him a hand, seeing how he was still under the weather.

As the week got closer to the end, Morgan got stronger with the fusion having been completed. With the others help, they were ready to receive Jack Daniels, and the mare.

"How are we doing so far?" he called out, as the owner of the thoroughbreds was about to drive in with his precious cargo on board.

"Pretty good!" Nate called back, when turning to see the long, black, shinny horse trailer pulling in. "Hey, heads up...! They're here...!"

With Jason's men standing at the ready, in case of trouble, Jason double checked his service revolver.

"Jason, are you okay?" Morgan asked, looking his way.

He nodded, and looked to his undercover officers. "Men, how about the rest of you?"

Showing their concealed weapons, they each smiled, knowing Copeland's reputation.

"Good. Morgan, we're all ready," he turned back.

"All right," he said. "Once we get these two settled in, we will be adding in a few more horses to blend in, along with them, so they won't stick out as much."

"That reminds me," Nate walked up to join him, "the other day I had gotten a call out at

this man's place, just north of here. He has a wild stallion, which needs taming. I thought if you didn't mind, we could have him brought here for Jade to work on."

"Just how wild are we talking?" he asked.

"Well, let's just say that I should be here with a tranquilizer ready in case he were to get out of hand."

"Great. Let's have the guys work with him, before letting her anywhere near the beast."

"My sentiments exactly," Nate agreed.

Days later, after receiving the horse, there was no keeping her from the shiny black stallion, which stood fifteen and a half hands tall. With rope and halter in hand, she let herself into the round pin, while everyone else was busy doing their work around the place. Meanwhile, having just closed and latched the gate to the corral, Jade hung the halter on a post nearby, and turned to the wild stallion with only the coiled rope in hand. "Okay, boy, let's see what you have, before I begin my work with you," she gently spoke, while keeping her movement slow and steady, while approaching him.

Getting up to him, she carefully raised the hand with the rope in it to see what he would do, while holding her free hand up and out to one side, with open palm facing him.

Rearing his head back, he took off running from her.

"Ahhh... I see!" she grinned mischievously. "So you want to play hard to get, huh?"

Snorting his response, he went on softly galloping around the ring, turning back and forth to avoid her roping him.

Meanwhile, uncoiled the rope, she tied a loop in one end, before lassoing it in the air.

Stopping, he looked at her, and began his pacing again.

"La, la, la, la, la, la, la..." she sung a tune, her mother used to sing her, while waiting for the right moment to catch him. When then she did, with the first throw. "Good, boy," she praised him, and reached into her pocket for a congratulatory treat to reward his good behavior. "Now let's see if you will let me put the halter on you, as well. Okay, Thunder," she called him.

Going to retrieve it off the post, he followed her to get more treats. Knowing this, she pretended not to, while letting him get to know her a little better, since they were going to be working so closely together.

Laughing, she turned with halter in hand, and reached into her pocket to get him another treat. "Well, I'll give you this. But you have to let me put this halter on you too. Are you going to be good for me?" she asked, looking softly into his eyes.

Again, he snorted and nodded his head.

"Well, okay. But just this time. I only brought three baby carrots with me. That's all the work I was going to do with you today."

While he ate it, he let her slip the roped material over his snout, and then over his ears, once he smelled it. Soon he was set to have a long lead rope attached to it, which she had laying over the gate from earlier.

"You are doing so well. Nevertheless, I do not want to read too much into it. So, I won't try getting on you just yet. I just want to lead you around the corral until you get used to having the halter on you. Tomorrow I will try a bridal. After that, I will add a saddle. When I think you have had enough time to get used to all that, I will get on myself, and just sit on you."

When the next day came, she did exactly what she said she would, and what better time. With Morgan out helping Nate with a delivery of a newborn calf, Jarred pretended to do old man

Copeland's bidding, while keeping tabs on what he planned to do. Jason on the other hand, continued to monitor the area for any possible trouble if Copeland were to send Bart out to do something Jarred was aware of.

Back in the ring, Jade lured Thunder up to her, by bribing him with a carrot, so she could tie him to a rail and brush him out, before their real work. "That's it, boy, we're not going to do anything real big today," she continued to talk to him in her soft, silky-like voice, to keep him feeling calm. "I just want you to get used to me, still. Is that so bad?" she smiled, while gently running a free hand over his neck and mane. Doing so, she had pictured herself hopping onto his back and riding him, until he finally broke to having her weight on him. But then, knew better to think it, when he gave her a toss of his head.

"Okay, so maybe that was a little premature on my part. Still what a thought," she laughed, getting his bridal ready to put on, while still having his halter on so she could work around it without him taking off on her. Once the bridal was in place, she would slip the halter off beneath it.

As for the rest of the day, it went by smoothly, when Ramsey came out to watch her. By then, she was ready to try the saddle.

"Are you sure he is ready for that?" her grandfather cautioned.

"No...! And I won't know if I don't try!"

"All right, but if you are going ahead with it, be careful not to be where he will plow you over with his big hooves. Morgan will have my hide if you get hurt now. Not to mention, no one is here if you were to get seriously hurt."

"Grandfather, you worry too much. I have been at this for so long, nothing has ever gone wrong yet. Now let me do what I do best, and get this saddle put into place, and off again, before master Morgan catches me out here doing this," she roused, pulling the large, leather saddle off the rail it was sitting on.

Holding onto the horse's reins, while his granddaughter preceded to do what she wanted, the horse reared his head anyway, and started dancing around, not liking what she was doing.

"Whoa, Thunder," Ramsey insisted, while offering a chant to help calm him down.

Soon it had worked, but only long enough to set the saddle on his back. After that, he was jerking and twisting all over the place, wanting the thing off him, until it fell off, after she jumped the fence to get out from being trampled on.

"Fine. We won't do that now. But you are going to have to get used to it sooner or later," she groaned, looking down at her watch. "Oh, Lord, I have better be getting this stuff put up, before Morgan *does* get back and sees what I have been doing!"

"Let me help," her grandfather offered, not taking no for an answer, when he saw the familiar look come over her then.

"Fine. Just take his reins, and pull him out of the way, so I can get his saddle. After I get it taken back to the tact room, I'll switch out his bridal for his halter."

Getting it all taken care of, she gave Thunder a carrot, and thanked him, before she and her grandfather went off to do some minor work on her room addition.

"He knows what you are wanting to do," her grandfather warned, having seen the look in the stallion's eyes.

"What are you saying? Don't do it? Just stay off him, and pretend Morgan and Cynthia will be happy as they are?"

Fighting the tears that threatened to fall, he didn't want to face the vision that he had had the previous night. A vision for telling that the time was getting so much closer for her to full fill her destiny. That night though he chanted his usual chants, hoping to bring things to a peaceful end for all those involved.

The following evening, while Morgan and a few of the guys were seeing to one of the horses in the stable, Jade went out to throw herself up on Thunder's back. Angry after the heated talk she and her grandfather had the previous night about the horse, she wanted to prove she had control over the beast.

Feeling her weight, he bolted hard, as she held tight to his mane, before being tossed off. Again, she jumped on, and again she was tossed off, only this time into a fence rail.

"Ouch..." she cried, getting herself up to stumbled off to one side to clear her head. But then, she heard several footsteps running her way. "Oh, great," she grumbled. "Just what I don't want to hear right now."

"What the hell...?" Morgan yelled, running from the stable, after seeing to another horse Nate had brought out to him. "What do you think you were doing...?" he yelled again, while signaling one of the guys over to restrain the animal. "You could have gotten yourself killed, doing a crazy thing like that. Besides, I had left strict orders that you were not to be working with him, until we have warned him down by working him our selves!"

"Yes, but it's my job," she groaned, wiping herself off, while walking up to the gate to come out. "Besides, if I want to kill myself, I will!"

"Not here, you won't," he growled down at her. Then it occurred to him, what Ramsey told him earlier. And now what she had just said.

"Yes," she glared back at him, "I know of your loss. And I know that there can only be one way for her to come back to you. So, let me do my job. If I get killed just be there to make
the switch, before she loses out on the opportunity to be with you."

"Wh...what...? No...!" he cried, shocked to the core. "You are out of your mind if I let you just throw your life away like that."

"But it's my life. And it is my decision how it ends."

Shaking his head, he turned sharply and walked away. Then, seeing Jason, he ordered him to keep her out of the corral, and away from the horse, until they could control him better.

Hearing this, she stormed off for the bunkhouse to get cleaned up, since it was getting late, and everyone wanted to call it a night.

Chapter Twenty

Later, while out walking the grounds with Cynthia by his side, Morgan told her what had happened out at the corral. "She's crazy. I know she is hurting over the loss of her parents. But suicide? Come on."

"She's obviously missing them. And how they were killed, she must be blaming herself for it."

"I can see how she would feel badly for that, since Copeland had warned her to pull back. After all, it was her he was after, and not them, after killing the horse."

"Morgan," She turned to look up into his eyes, "you know what this means, don't you?"

"You would have a chance to come back to me? Yes, and damn it to hell, I want you back. But for it to happen to someone I know!"

"Yes, I can see how it would bother you," she sighed heavily, "I was just missing our time together, is all."

"Me, too," he grinned coyly, while allowing his eyes to drift down to her breasts, before returning to see her warm expression looking back at him.

Later that night, while Jason and Nate grabbed some sleep, four of the undercover officers were keeping watch over the area. Meanwhile, while up in his room, Morgan laid sleeping, while Cynthia's mind was working overtime on how much she wanted him. By then, she was feeling the heat rise in her own body, so-to-speak, as she attempted something she hoped would get his attention.

'*A kiss, a feathery light one,*' she thought. Although, not being all that experience at making such a move, she found it harder to do.

Concentrating all her energy on getting him to feel something, it worked, as he began to move.

"No..." she murmured softly. "Please don't wake up!"

She blushed at the thought of him seeing her being so forward. Then, hearing his breathing return to normal, she began again. This time she went for the dark wisp of hair on his tanned chest. Afterward, the rest seemed easier, as she found him slowly becoming aroused at the attention she was attempting to give him. Thus, closing her eyes, she contemplated what to do next, when his hand went to run over his stomach.

"Mmmm..." she moaned at how he moved, and then she too repeated what he had done. Only as she did, he felt the tingling sensation when her hand reached the dampness of his skin.

"Oh... Muffet..." he groaned, when the name reached her senses.

Looking up, she saw his eyes gazing upon her now.

"What are you trying to do to me, little one?" he grinned.

"Only this," she replied, as the part of her that remembered what it was like for Cat, attempted to go on even further.

"Oh, God, you are not..." He breathed in the pain it was causing him. But at the same time, he found the experience to be very electrifying, as she continued to love him in a way she had never known before. "Oh... girl..." he felt the release about to hit, when he went to stop her. But then, having forgotten, his hand passed right through her. "Muffet, darling, you ha...have to stop... now," he cried, as things were coming even more to a head than before. "P...please... st...st...stop...!"

Hearing him, she became worried that she was hurting him somehow. But then, as she pulled back in time to see his fountain shoot out its worth, she cried, "Oh, my! Is that why you wanted me to stop?" she cried shamefully.

With one hand over his forehead, laughing to himself, he nodded his reply, as he went to get up to clean up the mess she caused him. "You are so mean to me, you know that?" he chuckled from across the room, before turning back to see her.

"Y...you... didn't like it...?" she whimpered sadly.

"Huh, like it? Are you kidding? When Cat did that to me, she would forever drive me out of my mind."

Smiling, she watched him take the time to straighten up the bed, before getting back in.

"Come, lay with me for as long as you can," he motioned with one outreached hand.

Doing so, he soon fell off to sleep, just as she had gotten a little more comfortable. But then something began to beckon her, as she got up carefully so as not to wake him.

Going out to see what it was, she found herself in the meadow, heading for the bunkhouse, while back inside, her father had just made his appearance in Morgan's room.

Upon hear him calling out to Cat, Thaddeus became alarmed at someone else's name coming from his lips. "Cat...!" he growled beneath his breath, as he looked around to see if someone else was there with him. Not seeing anyone, he peered back at the man laying there, naked, in bed. "*Who is this, Cat?*" he asked, glaring down at him. Seeing how this wasn't going anywhere, and not liking his lack of apparel, he turned and left the room.

Once out in the hall, he went in search of his daughter. A search that led out to the edge of the meadow, where she was slowly heading for the bunkhouse.

Suddenly, feeling his overpowering presence, she turned, instead of being afraid of him, she was actually happy. Still, though, something was beckoning her to come.

"What is it, child?" he asked in a more normal tone, as he came closer to see her expression.

"I don't know! I just feel drawn somehow, somewhere."

"This man up in his room, does he have something to do with this?"

"Oh no, daddy, he's wonderful!"

"Wonderful, huh? Then who is this 'Cat', he was calling out to, when I was up there just now?"

"Cat?" she repeated.

"Yes. Is she another woman, coming in between you two?"

"Oh, good heavens, no. That was *his* lost love. She too died like the rest of us, in child birth."

"Oh, but of course," he nodded, realizing his mistake.

Just then, his own senses became acutely alert to some kind of danger in the area, as he shielded her to see what it was.

"Daddy? What is it? What's wrong?" she cried fearfully.

"There are other men here."

"Yes. They are here to watch over the thoroughbreds back in the last stable."

"No. I know of them. This is a whole other group. Four to be exact. Moreover, they are not here to watch over anything. They wish to do harm to two of them."

"You know about the race horse, and the mare?"

Looking to his daughter, "I know everything that has been going on around here. These men mean trouble. And they have to be stopped."

"I have to warn Morgan, then!" she cried without thinking to call him Michael.

"No time to. You have to go to the bunkhouse, now! When you get there, get the one's called Jason, Jarred, and Ramsey up. And you must do it now, child. Hurry."

"Daddy, I am not a child anymore. Furthermore, I can't believe you actually want me to do this."

"Yes, and I know that I have been overbearing, when it came to you. I am sorry. Now get the fire under your tail, girl, and move it!" he laughed, as he was about to have some of his own fun with the trespassers.

"Daddy... wait...!" she called out, seeing his mischievous grin. "Just what are you going to do?"

"Teach those men a lesson," he returned, while leaving her to do just that.

Going to the bunkhouse, straight away, she went directly to Ramsey's bunk, first, and began calling out to him, "Oh, please wake up...!" she cried, before trying one of the others.

When she did, the door to the room opened, and Ramsey's granddaughter was standing in it. "It's you!" she murmured softly, so as not to scare her.

"Me...?" she questioned, with a hand to her chest, while looking back on at the girls' grandfather.

"Yes. And yes that is my grandfather that you are trying to wake, but why?"

"There are some men out there who are here to hurt the horses!"

"Oh, Lord..." she cried, reaching the short distance to her grandfather's bunk to shake him, "Grandfather...!" she called out to him. "Grandfather! You must wake up!"

Just then they heard his muffled voice, as Jason too woke to the sounds in the room.

"What's going on?" he asked, rubbing the sleep from his eyes.

Looking to Cynthia, Jade knew if she didn't say something, she may fade away, and in doing so, she would lose the chance to communicate with her spirit. "Please, once we get them out of here, I must speak to you. It concerns Michael."

"Yes, so he has told me of your loss."

"Will you stay so that we can talk?"

"S...s...sure! But first we must hurry, Father is already out there stirring up his own trouble."

"Thaddeus?"

Hearing the name, Jason and Ramsey shot up out of bed, as the lights went on, scaring Cynthia away. However, not far, as Jade turned looking for her, she saw her, as she was just about to leave. Getting her attention, she motioned for her to wait in the other room, just as Jarred came walking in.

"What's going on?" he asked.

"That's what we are wanting to know," Jason returned, while at the same time looking to the blonde, who was trying to hide what she was just doing. "What about Thaddeus?" he asked sharply.

"He's outside chasing off some bad men."

"What...?" Jason cried, grabbing up his service revolver. "But how do you know that?"

Looking to her grandfather, she swallowed hard, "His daughter was just here trying to wake you, Grandfather. It seems that Copeland's men are here to hurt the horses."

"But how did he know that they were here?" Jason continued, baffledly, while getting the rest of his things on, before heading out.

"Never mind that." Jarred had his own idea how. "Why hadn't I heard from Scott on it?" he growled.

"Unless." Jason looked to him worriedly.

Turning, both Jason and Ramsey called out to the others who had joined their merry band to protect the horses, while Jarred ran out to get into his vehicle to find his friend.

"I'll be right back," he called out, as he shoved the Bronco into gear, and peeled out of there.

Meanwhile, while everyone was out searching for the trespassers, Jade went in search of Cynthia. Finding her in the other bunkroom, she walked in carefully to take a seat on her bed, just as Cynthia turned back to face her.

"You are wanting to join your parents, aren't you?" Cynthia asked, surprisingly.

"Does that shock you?"

"A little!" she replied, while walking over to join her.

Feeling a little uneasy at first, Jade sat looking right into her eyes, and saw how much it would mean to her to be with Michael and have the babies they were meant to have.

"I have seen a vision of my parents. They are calling to me."

"You are an Indian, like your grandfather?"

"Half, but he has taught me their way of life, and these vision are real."

"Then what is it that you want from me?"

Telling her what she knew, the two went on talking, while up at the house Morgan was awakened by Brenda, when the call came in about the trespassers.

"I'll get dressed and go right away. However, call Steve and tell him we may need him. And then get your mom up to stay with you, while I'm out."

"Sure thing," she agreed, going right over to her mother's room to get her up while making the call.

Meanwhile, Steve and his family, on the other hand, were at their new house getting settled in, when the call came in.

Back at the bunkhouse, Jason and Ramsey each headed for the stables.

"Ramsey," Jason called out, on his way to the third stable, "you get this one," he pointed to number two, "while I get the third one."

"All right. You be careful," he called back, running for the second stable, while Jason took out his radio to call his men, and warn them.

Meanwhile, reaching the last stable, Jason found the two priced horses sleeping peaceful in their stall. Seeing this, he reached for the intercom. "Ramsey...!"

Hearing him, once he had hit the floodlights, he went right over to answer his call.

"Any trouble over there?" he asked, while reaching for the fuse box to turn on the outer lights, as well.

"No, and you?"

"Everyone is here and accounted for."

Before telling him the same, Ramsey heard a man cry out from the backside of the building, as another man threw a powerful right hook, sending him into the wall.

Back at the other stable, Jason's men walked up with two others in tow. Nonetheless, not wanting to chance their seeing the thoroughbreds lying in their stalls, they stayed outside to see what was to be done with them.

As for Morgan, having been the one Ramsey heard behind stable, beating the man he had caught sneaking around, when coming out to lend a hand. With Ramsey's help, he hauled him down to just outside the last stable.

When getting there, seeing a black backpack on one of the other guys' back, he handed his prisoner off to one of the officers, to go and get it.

To his surprise, there were two filled syringes in it intended for the horse. "Well, what do we have here?" he asked, looking back at the man who had been holding the bag, who was then in handcuffs, along with the other two.

"We aren't talking," they cried more nervously than usual.

"Oh? And may I ask just what are you doing here, then?" Morgan asked, when recognizing the red head, who had been holding the bag. "You...!" he thundered. "Where is the other guy...?" he demanded.

"He," the red head knew who he was referring to. "He got caught calling..."

Kicking him hard, one of the other guys told him to shut his mouth, "Unlessin' you want the same thing to happen to you."

Looking around to see who all was there, it was then Morgan didn't see Jarred amongst the group, and became greatly alarmed.

Seeing this, Jason shook his head. "It must be one of his friends, he's referring to," he offered, not wanting to say Jarred's name, because the others may squeal on him.

"Fine," Morgan growled. "It's off to jail for you three."

"That's better than what we have waiting back at the…" the third guy stopped.

"Circle C?" Morgan asked. "So am I to presume that your boss is back?"

"No. But his gorilla is, and he's bad news."

"Bart, you mean?" Ramsey asked, suspecting him to be the one behind the whole show in his son's accident, and the horse being killed.

"Yeah," they all said together.

"Oh, hell," Morgan groaned, as he turned his back to speak more privately to the two. "Jarred said he was growing more and more suspicious of him and Scott."

"Do you think the two may be in some sort of trouble at this moment?" Ramsey asked.

"One way to know for sure!" he said, taking out his cell phone to make the call. While waiting, he asked them one more question. "Where is Bart right now?"

Looking to each other, they shook their heads, but not the red head. Without giving himself away, he shakenly nodded off toward the woods to his right.

"Here?" Morgan mouthed the words so not to be heard.

The red head shook his head.

Meanwhile, the wait for Jarred wasn't long, when just then, his voice came over the other end, as he arrived to find his friend out back in a tool shed, awaiting his doom, after having been chloroformed, tied and gagged.

"Jarred," Morgan spoke quietly into the phone, "where are you?"

"Rescuing my friend. They had him knocked out, and stuffed in one of the back tool sheds."

"Is he all right?"

"Yeah. He's coming to now."

"Well, get him, and get the hell out of there. Bart is back. He's out in the woods, here, somewhere. Oh, and Jarred, drop him off at the house, Steve should be there soon. He can look him over, while you hightail it back out here to give us a hand."

"We're on our way," he returned.

Hanging up, he helped his friend out of the shed, and then over to the bunkhouse to grab their things and run. But before making their getaway, Jarred stopped and move a board from beneath his bunk that hid a journal he kept on everything Copeland and Bart had ever done. And with it was a list of all those the old man had on his payroll.

After getting it, they heard someone up at the main house coming out on the back deck.

"Who the heck would that be?" Jarred asked, peering out one of the front windows, in the dark to see a familiar face.

"Copeland!" Scott cried quietly, while looking over his shoulder. "What do we do now?"

"We get the hell out of here," he replied, while hauling their things out the back way to the Bronco, with Scott bringing up the rear. "You all right?" Jarred called back in a whisper.

"Yeah, I just have a mother of a headache, thanks to Bart."

"Tell me about it after we get out of here."

Just then, Jarred stopped in his tracts, when hearing what sounded like a phone coming from the main house. When turning from a squatted position, he saw Copeland go back inside to answer it. At that moment, he knew there was no time like the present to hightail it out of there, but quietly, so not to draw any undue attention to themselves.

"Damn, I thought he was gone still," he growled, while getting into the Bronco to head out the back way.

"He was, but someone called and told him that they hadn't seen you for awhile. That, and

I had been giving out the orders while you were out."

"Red, I bet."

"Yeah. And when I heard about the hit going down, Bart saw me about to call you."

"So he way laid you to keep you quiet?"

"Until he knew what he was going to do with me when he got back."

"Thank God for Cynthia and her father, then."

"What...?"

Laughing, he told him all that happened, before he left to come and find him.

"You are talking about Thaddeus Morgan, you know. He doesn't help anyone, but himself."

"He does if it's being done on his property, or to the ones he loves!"

"Great. So, we have a bad ass ghost to protect the place now," he laughed.

Chapter Twenty-One

Approaching the front drive of the Morgan Plantation, they saw three police cars and numerous K-9's out searching for the ringleader.

Getting clearance to drive on in, Morgan was the first to be seen, then Jarred's mother and sister, who had heard about Scott's detainment.

"Scott...?" Brenda cried out, as he got out to go to her. "Oh, Scott, are you all right...?" she asked, throwing her arms around him.

"I will be when I can sit down...!" he groaned, rubbing his head.

"Morgan," Jarred spoke up, "he took a heavy hit of chloroform, and now..."

"He has a splitting headache?" he laughed.

"Yeah. Can you help him?"

"No, since I don't have anything here, but I think..." he was about to say, when he saw his friends come out to join them. "Steve..." he called out, "do you have anything for a Chloroformed induced headache?"

"Perhaps a vitamin B-12 shot, but to tell you the truth, only an ice pack would help that."

"Mary...?" Morgan turned.

"I'll get one made up for him right away," she offered, while hurrying into the house.

"Thank, God, they're here and all right," Jarred groaned.

"You're not kidding," Morgan agreed, looking to Ramsey, who hadn't said a word, since coming up to the house with them. "Ramsey, what is it?"

"I'm worried about my granddaughter. He would be after her next, if he knew she was here."

"Where is she now?" Jason asked, looking around at all the faces.

"Still at the bunkhouse, where I had told her to stay."

"Oh, dear God," Morgan looked to the others. "With Bart on the loose, he may find her there."

"I hear you, buddy. We have to get her out of there, and now!" Jason ordered, while radioing a few of his men who were still in that area. "Ryan...!"

"Here," the man called back.

"Are you still near the bunkhouse?"

"Yes. Dave is here, too."

"Good!"

"Is that your best men?" Morgan asked right off.

"Two of them! Why?"

"Because, I have seen this Bart, and he doesn't waste any time with guys who can't hold a candle to him. Jarred," he turned, "it's up to us to go and get her. We both know this man, and I know you can take him on if you had too."

"You, too!" he grinned, thinking about the first day he had encountered him.

"Now wait a minute," Jason began to protest. "The two of you are big and powerful, but we are talking about a killer here."

"Yes, and one who will kill again if we don't get moving," Morgan glared. "As for the horses, has anyone seen them yet, outside of us that is?"

"No. We have the other guys out there keeping an eye on them now!" Nate announced, as the two began to head out for the bunkhouse together."

"Good. Keep them there," he called out over his shoulder, when they reached his Tahoe.

Getting in, the two were just about to start out, when Jason turned to Ramsey.

"Go with them," he said with a nod.

"Morgan...! Hold up. I'm coming with you."

Soon they were off an arriving at the bunkhouse with no time to waste. As the three got out, the two undercover officers greeted them.

"She's still inside," Ryan offered, while opening the door for them.

Going in, Morgan caught sight of Cynthia, who then turned to Jade, smiling.

"Miss Ramsey," he went on into her room to get her, "your grandfather is beside himself with worry over you. Shall we get you out of here?"

Looking back to Cynthia, she looked worried that she wouldn't take her up on what they had been talking about.

"Go," she whispered, so that only Jade and Morgan could hear. "I'll be nearby if you need me."

'Cynthia...' he shot her a puzzling look.

"It's all right," she continued to smile, but sadly now, as the girl left with the others.

"*Yes, but what was that about?*" he asked anyway, while hanging back.

"Do you recall what we were discussing earlier?" she asked, lightly.

"Refresh my memory."

"She is wanting to be with her parents. Oh, Morgan, what was I to say? You were right, it is crazy what she is thinking."

"Did she happen to say what is going to happen that might end her life?"

"No, but I can tell you this, it will indeed be an accident, since she knows taking her own life won't get her in to be with her parents. Though she won't go to... Well, you know."

"Yes," he grinned. "As for now, where is your father? I heard he's out here somewhere."

"Oh, yes, that he is," she smiled, while nodding her head out toward the stables. "He is making absolute certain that this other man is not going to get anywhere near the horses."

"Or near Jade, I hope. Because her life is in danger of this man, too, from what Ramsey says."

"I will certainly tell him that."

"You are all right with him now, aren't you?"

"Yes, ever since he has come around to accepting you."

"Good. Now I had better be getting you two back to the house."

"Don't worry about me, I will be there shortly."

"After you go and see your father?"

"Yes."

"All right," he replied, as he was about to tell her to be careful, but then laughed, while walking out.

Back at the house, once everyone was present and accounted for, the police stayed around with their guard dogs to watch over the area, until morning, when the Commander came out personally to see to the situation from the previous night. In the meantime, while everyone was talking in the parlor, Mary busied herself in the kitchen with Christy's help, prepared enough food to last out the rest of the night.

"Jason," Jarred spoke up, "something tells me that you are not just Morgan's friend, coming to give him a hand here. Am I right?"

"No, I'm not," he replied, as Jarred got up to hand him a black book.

"What's this?" he asked, looking at it puzzledly.

"You will find in there everything the old man had been doing, as well as Bart."

"And a list of who he has in his back pocket?" he asked, looking to Morgan, as a grin broke out, just then.

"Yeah. Now, I'm right, aren't I, about why you are really here?"

"Tell him," Morgan said, while coming over to look at the black book for himself.

"Yes, I am more than just a friend. I'm a cop, as well. I transferred down here to stop this Copeland from killing another racehorse. And now, Ramsey's granddaughter as well, from what I hear."

"Yes, since he missed and got her parents by mistake," Ramsey offered.

"Oh? Then I think you are all going to want to hear this," Jarred announced. "The old man is back. It seems that he was called, and told about my being gone so much, while leaving Scott, here, in charge."

"Any idea who?" Morgan asked.

"Red," Scott offered.

"Red? As in the red headed guy from the road incident? The same guy that was just taken in along with the other two we caught out at the stables?" he laughed.

"Yes," Jarred grinned.

"Speaking of Red," Jason piped in. "Just as they were about to take him away, he kept mumbling something about seeing Thaddeus's' ghost just after talking to Bart out in the woods."

"Oh...?" Morgan said, just as the others roared out laughing.

"Yeah! He insisted that the man they bumped into, turned and walked right through an old oak tree, as big as you and I put together, Morgan!"

"I don't doubt it at all!" he continued laughing, even when Mary walked in to announce food was ready in the dining room.

Getting up, everyone filed in one by one, while keeping the conversation light around the table in hopes, they would be able to sleep peacefully for the remainder of the night, knowing they were all guarded well.

As for Morgan, going up to his room, he found Cynthia standing at the window, looking out, as he walked in.

"How are things with your father?" he asked, closing the door behind him.

"Fine. I told him about Jade's life being in danger. He said he would watch over her, as well."

"And if what we have learned about her, comes true? Does he know about that, too?"

"No," she replied, when turning to face him, "I couldn't bring myself to tell him."

"Well, I have to admit, having him around now makes me happy. Especially if she..." He stopped at what he was about to say.

"I know what you're thinking, that she is so young, and smart about horses. What would I know about them?"

"Why, whatever we can teach you. Besides, what did I know, until Michael became a part of my life?"

"But we have the races coming up soon. What if..." she cried, while attempting to turn away, when he stopped her.

"No. Let's just hope that she doesn't get hurt by then," he suggested, when then seeing something else in her eyes. "Cynthia, what is it? What else has you troubled?"

"A part of Cat has been coming through again."

"Which part?"

"Her friend, Brenda. And when I saw her downstairs earlier, I wanted to go to her. Why is that?"

"Because, she and Cat had been really close."

"Were they..."

"Like sisters? Yes."

"Then, I should see her."

"When?"

"Tonight."

"As in right now?"

"Uh huh!"

"All right!" Taking out his phone to call Jarred, hoping he was still down in the parlor talking to Jason about the black book. Soon he had his answered.

"Yeah?" he answered gruffly.

"Jarred, it's me, Morgan. Is your sister still up?"

"Yeah, she's right here. Why?"

"Tell her that I need to see her. And that it's really important. And Jarred," he looked back to Cynthia, "tell her that it can't wait."

"Sure!" Getting off the phone, he looked across the room at his sister and Scott, cozying up in front of the fireplace. "Sis?"

"Yes?" She turned, looking over at him.

"That was Morgan. He wants to see you. He says it's really important, and that it can't wait."

"Mom...?"

"Go. See what he wants," the woman said, sitting in a comfortable, wingback chair.

"Scott...?" Brenda turned.

"I'm not going anywhere. I'll just be right here nursing my headache," he teased, acting like a baby.

Getting to her feet, she left the room to go up to Morgan's.

"Cynthia," Morgan turned back. "Are you sure this is what you want?"

"Yes. I can't explain it. I just know that I, or I should say, Cathy wants to talk to her," she was saying, while going over to get more comfortable on the bed, with her legs crossed, and her dress neatly situated over her lap.

Just then, there came a soft knock at the door, when Morgan went to answer it.

"Brenda. It's so nice of you to come. Please, come in."

"I don't understand! What is it that you want?"

Smiling, he extended out a hand to her. "It wasn't me exactly who asked for you. But if you'll just come in, I'm sure she can explain it better herself."

"She?" she asked, walking in as he went to close the door behind them.

At that time, looking from him, then around the room, her eyes lit up when seeing a smile on Cathy's face.

"Hello, Bren!" she spoke as clear, and as normal as she could, so not to scare her.

"C...C...Cathy?" she cried, while trying to decide to go to her, or flee the room.

"Yes, it's really me, girl. I just had to see you, and tell you how sorry I was for not having written more often."

"Oh, dear, Lord... it really is you, isn't it? But it's also Cynthia, too, right?"

"Yes, and it was just as I had told you, about living another life along time ago."

"Wow... and you have...! But why did you come back to this particular one? Why not clear back to when this curse had all begun?"

"Because they had someone that they were married to. Michael was taken from me and killed, just when our love couldn't have been more beautiful. So I was sent back here to wait for him."

"And now? Now that the two of you are together? What is stopping you from resting in peace?"

"We," Morgan came forward to explain, "weren't meant to have been torn apart in the first place. And now, with what has happened, we are meant to be together again. We just don't quite know how, yet."

"Wow... this is really beautiful! Will we ever get to talk again?"

"Oh, yes, you can certainly count on it," Cathy smiled wholeheartedly.

Saying her goodnights, the two met halfway to reach out their hands to each other.

"Goodnight, Bren...!"

"Yeah! Goodnight... Cath...!"

Seeing her out, Morgan turned back to his lady, and smiled, "We should be calling it a night too, you know?"

"Yes. Shall I leave you to be alone, or shall I..."

"Stay," he grinned. "But please, let me sleep!" he teased.

"Fine! Be that way," she returned playfully, while he went to pull down the quilt, before changing out of his clothes.

Chapter Twenty-Two

By morning, everyone was out working hard, when out of nowhere, came a black limo pulling into the driveway. Seeing it, Jarred grabbed onto Scott's arm, before letting Morgan know of their uninvited guest. Afterwhich, the two quickly ducked into the first stable to stay out of sight, as Morgan called to warn the others.

Sending a few good men up to watch over things, Jason watched through a pair of binoculars from a secluded spot along the lane, back to the third stable.

"Mr. Copeland," Morgan walked up, not once offering a friendly smile.

"Mr. Fairbanks, I just came to offer my apologies for last night's intrusion. I hope nothing was disturbed."

"No. But rumors have it that you are out to destroy two beautiful animals. So as a doctor and a veterinarian, I should tell you how wrong that would be. As for why your men were here last night, I would really like to know why, since all that I have here are strictly my horses. So, in a nutshell, you have no business coming around here, unless invited of course. And it's plain to see that you don't know the meaning of the word. So allow me to enlighten you." Flagging down the Commander, a man in his late forties, with graying hair, walked up, seeing the limo parked out near the stables.

"Mr. Copeland," he spoke up, reaching them, "I told you early this morning not to show yourself here again, as I had received two other complaints from Mr. Fairbanks on you before. Now, if you don't stop coming around bothering this man, we are going to have to serve you with a restraining order."

"Sorry. I had only come to offer an apology for my men being here last night."

"They wouldn't have been if you hadn't sent them!" Morgan growled.

"I did nothing of the kind!"

"Sorry, but that is not what I have on file from the report given last night. I have it on two accounts that you had specifically ordered four of your men to come here looking for one, Jack Daniels, and one mare, his mother, to have them killed so he can't run in the upcoming race. In fact, two filled syringes were found on one of your men who had given a sworn statement to that fact, just as we sent him off for a psychiatric evaluation, after what he had seen here."

"Oh? But then you couldn't hold his statement in a court of law. It would never wash after that."

"Perhaps not, but then we also have other incriminating statements to back it up. And at this time, I am not at liberty to say who had given them. But as of right now, you are hereby warned that you are under heavy suspicion. So, if I were you. And I'm not. I would stay clear of this place, and anyone connected to it, from here on out."

"Fine. Mr. Fairbanks," he said, turning red faced, "once again, I'm sorry." With that, the man turned to leave.

Not realizing it until then, Morgan thought it was strange that he hadn't noticed that Bart wasn't the one driving the limo just then, until the other chauffer got back out to open the man's door for him.

"Wait!" he called out stopping him.

"Morgan," Jason groaned, while still peering through binoculars.

"What happened to your other man, Bart?" he asked, throwing the old man off a little.

"Oh, I fired him late last night for drinking on the job."

"You mean because he fumbled up on not getting rid of one of your men that you had chloroformed and stuffed into one of your back tool sheds?" he corrected.

"Is that what you heard?"

"He was treated by a doctor, friend, of mine late last night at his clinic," he fibbed.

"Oh?" the Commander commented, while acting as though he didn't know. When that morning, the whole incident had been written down and given to him during breakfast, before everyone had started working.

Meanwhile, feeling as though the walls were closing in on him, Copeland denied everything and said his goodbyes, before making a hasty departure.

"So much for confessions!" they all agreed, while the others came out of hiding.

After another quick meeting with the Commander, everyone dove back into their work once again.

And with Morgan's back turned to the corral, where Jade and the others were working on the wild stallion, the black beast reared his front legs up angrily, while fighting furiously to break loose of the ropes holding him.

"Damn it, Jason...!" Nate yelled, while trying to sedate the animal. "Hold him for me."

"I'm trying, man...! But he's stronger than any of us can handle."

Just then, as Morgan went to turn and see what was going on, as the animal snapped one of the lines free, and began to charge blindly, not seeing Jade standing in its way.

"Jade_____!" Morgan shouted out, as he took one long leap over the fence to shove her out of the way. But he

205

was too late, as the animal plowed right into her, knocking her into a post, where her head hit with such force that she was no longer moving. "No_____!" he yelled, when at that very moment, the horse was about to charge at her again.

At Morgan's command, Jason and two other undercover men pulled out their revolvers and fired off a volley to stop the animal dead in his tracks, before he could reach her.

"Jade_____!" Morgan called out again, as now Ramsey was running out to see what all the commotion was.

Seeing his granddaughter lying still-like, he knew from their long talks and arguments the other night, her vision of seeing her parents was going to come true, thus giving her life over to Cynthia so she and Morgan can be together.

"Morgan," he spoke quietly, "you must go and get Cynthia. Now."

"What...?" he asked, turning to look up at the man's emotionless face.

"You heard me. Now hurry, as this is what she wanted for you and the young woman. So go and get her."

"But..." he started, when before he could move, Cynthia, having been out walking in her mother's rose gardens, came to see what was going on.

Walking up from behind, she replied in a ghost-like whisper, *"No, I'm here...!"*

"M...M...Morgan..." Jade came to, but only long enough to say her farewells. At that moment, she saw Cynthia's spirit standing off behind his broad shoulder.

"What is it?" he asked, sadly.

"Y...you're here...!"

"Yes," Cynthia whispered, as she went to kneel before her.

"T...take good c...care of him, and have lots of b...babies you and h...him."

"We will. Thanks to you," she cried, tearfully, as Jade turned then to her grandfather.

"Papaw, y...you must h...hurry now. I c...can't hold on much... lon...ger..."

"Yes, little one," he nodded, as Morgan ordered Nate to get the Tahoe.

"Hurry_____!" he shouted, while wasting no time to carry her out of the corral, and to the back seat of his vehicle, when it was brought around. "Jason, call Steve and tell him what had happened. Tell him too, that we are on our way."

"Sure will. Be careful driving," he called back, pulling out his phone.

"I won't be the one doing the driving. That will be Nate's job, as I will be riding in back, while keeping an eye on her. Ramsey, you *are* coming, right?" he asked, looking back at him.

"Yes, of course," he said, getting in.

As they rushed her off to the hospital with Cynthia by his side, Morgan, being careful on just how he put it, told his friend what had happened.

"That's obvious, we were all there!" Morgan exclaimed, then saw a glimmer of Cynthia sitting in next to him. "Oh, dear, Lord, I think I know where you are going with this. It's the chance for Cynthia to come back, isn't it? That explains what Jade was saying, before she passed out!"

"Yes, I am afraid so."

"But how?"

"From a vision she had," Ramsey offered, as he began chanting, to protect her spirit from any of those that are bad, from stepping into her if she were to leave, before they could get the transformation completed.

"And from that she knew she wasn't going to be with us much longer," Morgan added, sadly.

Listening in silence to the chanting, they got to the hospital, where Nate rushed in along with the others to find Steve standing by with a gurney and two nurses, one of which was his wife.

Giving him a brief run down on her condition, Nate pulled him off to the side to fill him in on the delicacy of what else was to go on.

"You're serious?" he asked.

"Very. You know the story. You saw it for yourself how Morgan has taken on Michael's memories. Well, now's the chance for Cynthia to come back to live out her life with him. Ramsey can even attest to it all. He was there, and heard it for himself. And Steve, she had even told Morgan."

"And Cynthia," Morgan spoke up, when he walked up, leaving Ramsey with his granddaughter, to see what the holdup was.

"Let's go then," Steve ordered. "We have no time to waste if we are to succeed."

Walking into the exam room, Nate turned to his friend, "It's up to you, buddy."

"What...?" Morgan asked, looking confused, when his friend then turned to Ramsey.

"You have to do this yourself," the old Indian explained. "It's the only way to get passed what had happened with your wife."

"And..." Nate stopped, as he felt really bad at seeing the anguish on his friends' face.

"No...!" He shook his head, backing away. "I...I can't...!"

"Yes, you can. And you must," Steve put in sympathetically. "For Catherine's sake, as well as for Cynthia and Michael's."

"But why me?"

"Because, you have to. So do it," Steve insisted harshly, knowing just how much he did not want to step foot into an operating room again. However, with his knowledge of the brain stem, he knew just how to relieve any swelling, if any had accrued in her accident.

"Besides," Nate chimed in, as he tried smiling, "we'll be here with you, all the way!"

"Sure, but this isn't what I had practiced! What if..."

"No," Steve cut him off, "and yes, you did work in the field of brain surgery for a short stint, before choosing to become an Obstetrian."

"Yeah, well that was only for a short stint, and that was then. Now, is now."

"Morgan," Ramsey took his arm, "she's counting on you. So don't let her death be for nothing."

Pondering over the though, he shook his head miserably, before heading in to get themselves ready. And as he said, Nate, Steve, and even Ramsey, with his doctrine, was allowed to be there for the surgery after all the X-rays had been taken to find the cause, and fix it.

Meanwhile, the second nurse had been sent out to prepare a room for when it was over.

And now as the surgery took place, Morgan fought hard not to think on what had taken place with his late wife, as his hands began the most crucial part of its job.

After hours of backbreaking work, Steve had finally asked how he was holding up, while

Christy went to wipe away the perspiration from his brow.

"F...ine," he grunted, as he gave a pair of sutures a toss, before being handed another pair off the tray. "Nate, I can use some light over here!"

"Where?" he asked, while quickly moving the stand around to help.

"Here," he indicated with a blood covered gloved hand. "Christy..."

"Another glove?" she asked promptly.

"Yes."

Turning away from the table, while Steve moved in to assist, the gloves were properly changed, and soon Steve stepped aside to allow Morgan back in. Meanwhile, Ramsey went on chanting, only this time to help set her spirit free, as the surgery was soon nearing its end.

Now, with everyone there to see the blessed event, along with Cynthia, Jade's spirit lifted itself free of its body and came face to face with the one who was going to take her place. "It's your turn," she smiled, looking then, to the others. "They're coming for me. I can feel them. And dear sweet Grandfather, be happy for me!"

"I shall, my little Running Horse. I shall." He cried for the first time since her accident.

"Morgan..." she turned," you have done well for a mere pale face. Be proud, and don't give up your practice forever, people out there need someone like you."

Smiling, he turned to Cynthia, who looked back to Jade, and with a knowing nod, she soon took the woman's place as the most brightest of lights, and the most beautiful, came from the heaven's with multitudes of angels along with it. Not to mention, Chief Ramsey's son and wife, to take their daughter home with them.

Saying her goodbyes, she parted company, and soon the light was gone.

Now the real wait began, as everyone stood by waiting and wondering when she would open her eyes.

"Morgan, it may be awhile," Steve murmured, quietly. "Let me get her to her room so the two of you can be alone. It's just up on the second floor."

Nodding his head, Steve went out to get a couple of orderlies to assist in moving her up stairs.

After getting there, Morgan didn't bother to get cleaned up, until he knew she was going to be all right.

Still they waited for yet another long drawling hour of listening to the monitors, as they let out short bleeps from time to time to indicate measures of her heart rate and brain activities. Though, while he sat quietly waiting, the others were out at the nurse's station keeping tabs on the monitors from there.

"Let's just hope it worked," Steve groaned, while listening off in a distance to Ramsey, as he carried on in quiet solitude.

"Yes, for Ramsey too," Nate added, sadly. "His granddaughter meant the world to him, as did his son and daughter-in-law."

Meanwhile, in the confines of her room, Morgan continued watching over her, as tears ran down his handsome face. "Come on, girl..." he groaned impatiently. "You have to wake up. Please...! Or how are we to have all those babies we've been talking about? That's if you don't kill me with all that energy of yours," he laughed. "So please wake up and say something. Anything. Please...! I need you. Do you hear me? I... need... you," he continued, while holding onto her hand.

At that moment, he lowered his head and began to pray, as he had never prayed before. As he did, something began to take place in front of him, as she began to squeeze his hand.

"Cynthia..." he cried, as he looked up to see her head moving to the side.

Seeing it on their monitors, as well, they came rushing in to hear her first moans.

"Mmmm..." she began painfully. "Oh, God... it hurts...!" she cried, opening her eyes to see his smiling face. "M...M... Morgan...?"

"Yes, it's both of us," he teased, including his, once, alter ego, Michael, while Nate and Steve moved around to check on her.

"Cynthia," Nate spoke up, while taking her pulse, "aside from the pain at the back of your head, how do you feel?"

"Mmmm... dizzy."

"That will pass, too," Steve offered, smilingly. "Though I must say, I can't believe it happened," he shook his head at Morgan. "She is really here!"

"Mmmm, where?" she asked, puzzledly, as her mind was still making the switch. "W...where am I?"

"You are still in the hospital," Morgan explained, while standing at her bedside. "Steve had you put into a private room, until we knew how you were going to be! And from the looks of things, I think you're going to be just fine!"

"Get some rest for now," Steve suggested. "By morning we'll see how you're looking."

"M...Morgan..." she began frightenedly.

"It's going to be all right. I'm not going anywhere without you. But I do need to get out of these dirty scrubs," he pointed.

Luckily for him, Christy walked in with his other clothes in hand so he didn't have to go far. Before she knew it, he was back to stay with her the rest of the night, while the others went back to the house.

"We'll see you in the morning," Nate called out from the doorway. "And remember, she needs her rest," he teased.

Shaking his head, Morgan let out a low growl, as the door went closed behind them, but then he went out to catch them before they could get onto the elevator. "Nate?"

"Yeah?"

"Where's Ramsey?"

"He went on back to the house just a little while ago. Something to do with the family ritual, of going off to be alone to do some other type of chanting to send off the spirit."

"Yes, I thought I had heard him out in the hallway," he nodded, as he turned to go back into her room and lie in next to her, while she slept throughout the night, until Steve came back later to check on them.

"How is she?" he asked, waking Morgan.

"Sleeping peacefully."

"Good, and what about you?"

"Tired, hopeful, and..." he looked to her, as he went to get up, "I'm so darn glad to have her, and all my friends around."

"Same here, buddy. Same here. Hey, I was just about to get some coffee, and since she is sleeping, why don't you come and join me?"

"No. But coffee does sound pretty good."

"In that case, I'll bring you back a cup, and we can talk then."

"Steve..." he called out quietly, as his friend was about to leave.

"Yeah?"

"How are things at the old clinic? Have you decided to stay there, or find a newer office, like we had talked about?"

"I haven't really thought about it. Why?"

Thinking about what Nate had said back during the funeral, it brought a smile to his face.

Then, too, what Jade had said, *'People need you.'* At that, he recalled Catherine saying, *'Don't give up.'*

"Morgan...? You all right?"

"Yes. I'm just fine."

The following day, after Cynthia's release, from then on, everything was working out wonderfully for them. The two were finally able to finish going through the rest of his things together out in the stable, while planning to put some of it in the Carriage House, and had even laughed over some of the other things.

Catherine's memories, unlike Michael and Morgan, who had joined to become one, she and Cynthia were always the same, as her spirit traveled, like it said, to find her intended love. Through it all, Cynthia was beginning to look more like herself, since they all shared the same hair and eye color throughout the line of Habersham's. Thus, bringing her and those who loved Catherine, closer together. People like Christy, Lacy, Brenda, and her mother, who have missed their Cathy. Now the couple was truly ready to tie the knot, with her father being there to see it take place.

The big horse race did go off without a hitch. Though, Copeland kept trying to kill Jack Daniels.

As for Bart, his body *was* found in an old abandoned mineshaft, with his hair somehow having turned an ash white. In addition, the look on his face was indescribable, as though he had seen... a Ghost?

~ Epilogue ~

Now married, the newlyweds are deliriously happy, while expecting their first daughter at anytime. As for Thaddeus, having welcomed his new son-in-law into the fold, he would prefer never to see Morgan naked again, as it was too frightening even for himself.

And now, as time was getting closer for the newest arrival, grandpa Ramsey and grandpa Thaddeus could not have been more excited. However, they were going to have to wait on that, since the grand opening of the newly renovated clinic came first. When that day had arrived, so did the celebration with the entire town folk, gathering around, as if with any celebration that took place in New Orleans, it was huge.

"Hey...! Are we ready...?" Morgan called out from the foyer, as he went to pull out a couple of raincoats for him and his wife.

"Yes. Yes. Yes," she groaned, while coming down the stairs, all big and round in the tummy. "You know you can't be rushing me now!"

"No, I suppose not, since you are about to drop at anytime now."

"Well, it can just wait. I have way too much to do, before then, and the nursery is just not quite ready. We still have to get up to the attic to get out mom's old crib and all the other things, which you, my dear husband, were supposed to be doing already."

Laughing, he shook his head. "So this is what being an expecting parent is like?" he roar

ed, as the others came out to join them. Scott with his pregnant wife, Brenda, who was also expecting a girl, and had planned to call her Catherine. As for Mary, the doting grandmama, she couldn't be much happier with how things had turned out.

As for Jarred, seeing Copeland in prison for, Lord knows how long was just the ticket. Not to mention, seeing the old man's son take over the Circle C., where together, with everyone else, cleaned up what the old man had done. After that, the people around there started to live more happily. Especially with the dirty cops and politicians out of office, replaced with goods ones.

And Brice, he too was living the life of bliss, having asked Mary to be his wife, as she had finally consented after a long time of contemplating the move. Still though, she remained Morgan's faithful cook, as Brenda chose married life over housekeeping anytime, while giving Morgan a hand finding himself a few more girls to fill her shoes.

"Morgan! Morgan!" Cynthia called out repeatedly to try and get his attention. "Honey, where are you?" she laughed, seeing the blank look on his face.

"Uh, what?" he asked, while pulling himself out of his deep thoughts, as the rain outside kept coming down in soft willow-like sheets.

"He's probably recalling the first time he had walked into this place, not all that long ago," Nate smiled fondly from the open doorway.

"I will never forget that day for as long as I live," he grinned down on his wife.

"Well, enough of memory lane," Mary uttered motherly-like, "Jarred and the others are waiting out in the cars to go now."

Helping her on with her raincoat, the crowd was soon out the door and in their designated vehicles, with Morgan taking the lead out of the long, tree-lined driveway, to the new medical clinic across from the animal hospital. In no time, they were there to celebrate the new opening, with a wide variety of food catered in from the public to say thank you for cleaning up all that had been done wrong to them.

"Well, guys," Nate spoke up, while holding up his glass of wine to toast their dream that had been planned since college, "here is to our success and many years of working together. May they be long and prosperous."

"Here. Here," Morgan agreed, while holding his wife in one hand and clinking glasses with the other.

It was then that seeing how Cynthia wasn't looking so well, Christy came up to take her aside, while the men went on talking amongst the patronage. "How are you feeling?" she asked, while finding her a comfortable place to sit awhile.

"Uh... like she's anxious to get out and join the living!" she groaned heavily.

"Any trouble with backaches or swelling?"

"Some backaches from time to time."

"When did they start?"

"This morning, why?"

"She could be getting ready to come, is all."

"I hope not! Morgan and I were planning to go out to the carriage house this afternoon to have another look around!"

"Well, just to be on the safe side, you had best take some warm blankets with you, in case she does decide to come."

"Yes, I..." she broke off frightfully all of a sudden, as the tears began to emerge.

"Cynthia, honey, what is it? Are you in pain now?"

"No. It's just that..." She went for a Kleenex, when a slip of paper fell from her pocket.

Picking it up for her, Christy saw a lot of dates and names on it. "What's this?" she asked puzzledly.

"Oh, it's the name and dates of each of the Habersham women along the line. Morgan brought it out for me so that we can find just the right name for our little girl!"

Opening it more, she pointed to all the different ones to explain their relationship to her. "This of course is the latest," she cried, covering her mouth at seeing the name inscribed, Christina Meghan Fairbanks 4-04-02 – 4-04-02.

"Oh, wow_____" Christy, too, cried, seeing the name, which was intended to be used after her own, "I remember the day you two had decided on that name."

"Yes, and we weren't so sure if we should tempt fate again, so he got out the records of my family and we began going through it. As you can see," she pointed out.

Name	D.O.B.	D.O.D.
Christina Meghan Fairbanks-	4-04-2002	4-04-2002
Catherine Kay Habersham-Fairbanks-	4-07-1969	4-04-2002

"The name Habersham was added when he found out about the family. Then Catherine's mother, Clarice Habersham-Cantrell, 7-16-1944 to 4-07-1969, Courtney Clarice Habersham-Bartlett, 6-18-1919 to 7-16-1944, and then Constance..." She then stopped upon seeing the name scratched out, and a new one replacing it.

At that time, Morgan was now standing at her side, as Christy moved away to let him in.

"Yes, Muffet, I had it done to the headstone, as well, with your father's permission, that

is. It now reads: Constance Maria, after my...Michael's mother," he corrected. "Habersham-Morgan-Fairington."

"That's so beautiful," Lacy replied, joining them.

"And the rest," he went on, while taking the paper from her trembling hand, "being named somewhat after her grandmother, 9-15-1894 to 6-18-1919, then Cynthia Constantina Habersham-Morgan-Fairbanks, once again being changed to the rightful name, born 3-07-1869 to..." seeing the date, even he had gotten choked up with emotion, as Nate then took the paper to read.

"9-15-1894. The next on the list is great-great-great grandmother, Constantina Elli Anna Habersham-Morgan, herself, born 1-28-1844 to 3-07-1869, then last but not least, great-great-great-great... grandmother Clarisa Ann Morrietti-Habersham, born 12-16-1824 to 1-28-1844."

"The beginning of the Habersham line," a woman sounded from the crowd that gathered round to hear the history of her family.

"Do we know you?" Morgan asked, looking from his wife to the old gypsy woman, now standing before them, in her red and yellow garment.

"Ask her!" she smiled sweetly to Cynthia.

Thinking for a moment, it came to her. "You were the lady in the library!"

"Yes. And now I'm here to tell you that the curse that my great-great grandmother placed on your fourth great is indeed over. As for this child you are carrying, she will be born happy, healthy, and full of life. And of course, as all beautiful women, a real heartache to most men."

Smiling, they thanked the woman as she slowly left the crowd, stopping though when she reached Ramsey. Smiling up at him, she whispered something in his ear as she turned back one last time to look upon the happy couple.

"I will see to it," he returned, thanking her.

After the celebration was over, the men joked about how Morgan was going to work at both clinics to help the other friend out.

"That ought to be interesting," he laughed, getting their coats for them again.

As he went to put it on her, she cringed at a severe back pain, just then, but hid it from him as they walked on out to the Tahoe.

Once home, he asked if she were ready for their walk. Although, despite the fact she was still feeling a great discomfort to her lower back, she didn't want anything to get in the way of their late March walk out to the carriage house.

"Sure!" she replied, tensely, while trying to hide the next pain from him. "But first, will you just run up and grab a few blankets, since it has gotten a little chilly out? Oh," she pointed up the stair from the open doorway, "grab that sack laying in next to the bed too."

Doing just that, he was back in no time, as the two went out through the rose gardens, and passed the broken-down, split-rail fence. Soon they were at the spot where he had recently put an opening in the fence so she could walk on through.

Grabbing onto the post, she cried out, feeling her water break. "Oh, dear, Lord_____! Morgan_____!"

"Right here, sweetheart. I guess it's about that time, huh?" he asked, seeing her eyes clinch tightly, as the next pain came even harder than the last.

"Yes_____ it sure looks that way to me_____!"

Looking to the front door, he figured he could get her inside, and onto the couch, once there. "Come on, let's see if we can get you at least to the couch."

"No... the bedroom where we first made love."

"But that's so far for you to have to go!"

"Just a few more feet_____! Please_____!" she cried, hanging tightly to his arm, until another pain passed.

"All right, fine. Let's try to make it that far."

In moments, he had her lying down on the freshly made bed. Surprisingly, a fire was already flickering in the fireplace.

"Are you comfortable?" he asked, hurriedly.

"Uh huh...!" she answered, while looking around the beautifully decorated room, with all its bright colors and old fashion quilts hanging on a nearby wooden stand. "Michael?"

He looked to her worriedly.

"It looks as though someone had been out here cleaning the place up. I know we have been here from time to time, but this is really nice. Even the flowers in..." She stopped to wait out the pain.

"Cynthia?" he asked, as he went to see how things were looking otherwise. "Good," he sighed, seeing how she was beginning to dilate, "I have just enough time to put on some water, and get whatever supplies I can use out here. "Oh, and Cynthia..." he called out from the living room, "I should call Ramsey and see if he could run me out a few more things to help this along! But first I had better get the water going." Having said that, walking into the ample sized kitchen with all its old style amenities, he saw just what he would be needing to deliver their baby, sitting by the sink, along the back wall. "What the heck? First the freshly made bed, then the fire, and now this?" he grinned, while going over to the counter to have a look. Along with it was a note, which was barely legible.

Morgan, it began.

You should find everything here that you will be needing.

However, if you feel you're in a bind, just call out, and someone will be there.

Ramsey

"Great. So you are a psychic, too."

Suddenly, hearing a scream from the other room, grabbing the equipment, he ran in to see her wanting to push. "No_____" he called out, going to her, "it isn't time yet."

"That's... what you... think_____!" she cried, pointing to the wet area on the bed.

Looking beneath the quilt he used to cover her with, his eyes went wide with surprise. "But, I just checked you, before going in to get some water on. How..." He stopped to see her smiling face.

"Like I said, she wants out."

Seeing the baby's head was already crowning, he ran back into the kitchen and started the water right away. "Okay, Morgan, you can do this, you're a doctor for crying out loud. So calm down now and think. Think, hell! That's our baby coming. Oh, Ramsey_____" he cried, "what am I to do_____?"

Meanwhile, just out at the stables, Ramsey looked up, just then, to see Thaddeus walk in.

"It's time," he nodded.

"The carriage house?" Ramsey asked, smiling.

With yet another nod, the two proud grandfathers were off to see the miracle of their granddaughter's birth. Though, worried about the history of the Habersham women, Thaddeus, known as an old tyrant, began to pray all the way there.

Upon walking in, Morgan turned to see one out of breath Indian, and one worried old sea Captain standing in the middle of the living room. "She is already crowning," he smiled, while taking in a pot of hot water for her. Just then, seeing the bag she had asked him to get for her, out of the corner of his eye, he stopped to hand back the pot to Ramsey.

"What is it?" he asked.

"The bag she had asked me to get for her."

Picking it up, he looked inside to see the baby's receiving blanket.

Smiling, he brought it in to her. "You knew, didn't you?"

"Uh huh."

"How long?"

"Since the party."

"And you didn't tell me?"

"Uh, uh."

"Why?"

"I didn't want anything to get in the way of what we had planned! I had hoped that we would have her out here! Right where..." she looked to her father, "we made love for the first... time...!"

Looking back to see he wasn't upset, Morgan turned back, "But still," he went on, while handing her the blanket, "you could have put yourself and the baby's life in danger, don't you know that?"

"Michael..."

"No, it's Morgan right now. And yes, Michael, but still, do you have any idea how much like Cat you are, by doing that?"

"And," she smiled coyly, "like myself."

"So I am beginning to see." He too smiled, as he couldn't help but shake his head at her.

At that time, their happy moment was about to be interrupted, as another hard contraction hit, bringing her up to push.

Just then, her father cried out, "What can we do?"

Laughing at his question, Morgan replied, "Well, she could sure use some cool water for her face, and..." Turning back to see the look of contempt, he just laughed even more. "All right, how about Ramsey get the water, and you, Thaddeus," he turned to look at his lovely wife, "go and have a seat next to your daughter. I think she would love having you here."

Doing so, the work truly kicked in, as Ramsey came around to help lift her into the pushing position, while she pushed with all she had, until little Constantina was born.

Hours later, after all was said and done, both mother and daughter were doing fine, while both grandpa's, teary-eyed and all, watched over them with such awe.

As for Morgan, after letting in her dog, who had recently started scratching and whimpering at the door, wanting in to be near them, had gone over to join his wife and child in what was sure to be, the most beautiful picture of all.